Contents

A LOVER'S *Heist* 3

BABY AND SKAI'S LOVE STORY

K.L. HALL

A Lover's Heist III: Baby and Skai's Love Story
(Heist of Hearts Series Book 3)

K.L. Hall

Synopsis

For as long as she can remember, Skai Daniels has wanted to be a surgeon. As a second-year surgical resident at a hospital in the heart of Miami, her budding medical career keeps her busy. All work and no play make for a lackluster social life. So, when she decides to spend her first night off in a week tagging alongside her best friend, Jade, to a private party, what's the worst that could happen? What starts as a fun night soon leads to a series of twisted events that throw her right into the arms of the youngest and notably most problematic Snow brother, Baby.

Cash rules everything around Judah "Baby" Snow. The young boss lives by the street code and runs with the meanest. With his heart still recovering from his last relationship, the paid and pretty playboy is rigid and temperamental. Emotions on ice, he's vowed never to make the same mistake twice until fate lands him in the middle of Skai's apartment, searching for his stolen possessions and answers she doesn't have. When their worlds collide, they'll learn they have more in common than expected.

As pulse-pounding sparks fly, will Skai crack the forbidden code to Baby's cold, wild heart, or will a ghost from his past get in the way of the future he could have with her? In a city with enemies at every turn, he could lose everything over the one thing he said he'd never do again, fall in love.

*Please note: This is the final standalone novel in the Heist of Hearts series. Each book in the series will feature a different member of the Snow family with no cliffhangers. *

Disclaimer

*"This is the heart of the tale I have always wanted to tell you.
The beginning of a fiery promise and the end of a devouring sorrow.
The all in all and the truth of the truth."*

-Christopher Poindexter

BABY

"If you be good to me, then I'ma be great to you. If you stay down for me, then I'll stay awake for you."

The 808's thumped to Chloe's *Surprise* as I watched Asian Bliss take the main stage. Blue-faced hundreds rained down from the sky as her heavily tattooed limbs twisted and folded around the chrome pole, defying gravity as she slid down into a split under the hot pink neon lights. With tats from her neck to her wrists and a head full of long, raven black hair, I admired how her warm beige body spun around the pole like a fuckin' ballerina. Niggas stood around, studying her with unwavering attention like they'd just been transported through time and space into a new multiverse where only she existed. She kicked her six-inch heels through the air, doing acrobatics while making her ass pop and jiggle like the crowd-pleaser she was. All the

1

Miami ballers and hustlers came to see her at The Sanctuary, a new, high-end Miami strip joint filled with the city's baddest bitches.

Years ago, it was called the Pleasure Palace before it got shut down after the owner got caught running an underground prostitution ring. It remained an abandoned warehouse on the city's outskirts until eight months ago, when someone bought it, rehabbed the shit out of it, and reopened its doors two months ago. What once was a rundown shithole was now the place where all the Miami ballers wanted to make it rain and sleet every day of the week, no matter if it was W.A.P. Wednesdays, Thicc Thursdays, or Fantasy Fridays. It was the type of place you could go to and have a full-course meal on the rooftop and then go downstairs to see bitches walking on the ceiling and asses and titties shaking and jiggling all over the place.

I turned my glass of 1942 up to my lips to fuel up for a long night of partying, G-string tucking, and paying for rent, tuition, and plastic surgeries alike. After her song was over, I moved through the crowd to the bathroom. The club was a jungle, just like every weekend, with niggas in there cappin' and frontin' at every turn, trying to convince these hoes they could change their lives and take 'em from the pole to the penthouse overnight. On my way back from the bathroom, I saw Asian Bliss and another stripper named Honey Moan talking as I made my way in their direction.

"Bitch, what you mean you can't go back out there?"

"I can't. I don't feel good."

Asian Bliss smacked her lips. "You know Bankx ain't gon' have that shit. You better get one of these other hoes to go out there for you!"

The babble of talk died as I inched closer. I blinked as my eyes adjusted after hearing the name Bankx fall off Asian Bliss' tongue. Usually, I heard little and cared less. To me, it was all gibberish until it wasn't. The sound of his name alone sobered my ass up real quick. I stopped dead in my tracks, locking my eyes on hers like a magnet. She raised her right eyebrow before her narrow maple-brown eyes squinted.

"Can't you see we talkin'?" she snapped.

Without saying another word, I pulled out a stack and gently slid it against the sparkling crystal tassels swinging across her glittery chest. Her red-painted lips turned up a fraction of an inch before she tilted her neck to the side, signaling for Honey Moan to leave us. Money was a universal language. For the right amount, I knew she'd dance on me like she loved me and would give me the information I needed if I played my cards right.

Once we entered the private room, I sat on the red velvet couch and watched Asian Bliss' body cling to the pole as if they'd been fused into one. Her light-up six-inch heels twirled around the shiny chrome before she hit the ground and started pussy poppin' like she was straight from the projects. After doing a round of acrobatics like the pole fairy she was, she stepped down from the platform and sauntered over to me.

"Is there room for me on that lap?"

"Always," I answered. "You know you da baddest in here, right?" I mumbled to her as she climbed on my lap.

She tossed her head full of long, dark hair back, revealing the spiderweb tatted across her throat. "Tell me something I don't know, daddy."

"I bet you got niggas in here wishing they could sniff the lining of those panties, huh?"

"Mmhm, but you, you might just be the exception," she informed as she drank me in with her sultry, thin-slit eyes.

"Damn, and you smell good too."

She gently brushed her hand against the septum piercing in her nose. "Trust me, daddy, I taste as expensive as I look."

"I bet you do," I implied before tossing a few hundred dollar bills her way. "Let me take care of you for the night."

"You wanna take care of me? I like the sound of that," she moaned before palming the back of my head while gyrating against me.

"Listen, my brother is getting married in a few weeks, and I'm in charge of the bachelor party. You and a few of your girls should fall through," I insisted.

"Mmm. Your brother as fine as you?" she purred, winding back against me like a yo-yo.

"Baby girl, ain't nobody fine as me," I assured her.

She smirked. "So, you wanna private party?"

I dipped my chin. "Yeah."

"How many girls?"

"As many as you can get."

"I can for sure get six girls. That's ten racks minimum upfront. Plus tips," she informed me.

"I can handle that, no question."

"Good. I'll set you up with Jamie at the front when we leave here. She'll get the date and information from you."

"Bet. So, uh, now that we got our business out the way, let's get back to you and me.

"What about us, daddy?" she asked, continuing to grind against my dick.

"How long you been working here?" I asked, toying with a lock of her hair.

She shot her eyes up at the camera over her left shoulder. "No touching, baby. Eyes are everywhere."

"My fault."

"I've been dancing for four years, but here, only since the club opened about eight or nine months ago."

"Mmm. Who owns this spot now? It's fire."

Something like a sigh pushed past her lips. "You wanna chit chat, or you want these perky ass titties in your face?" she asked with a twinge of annoyance, which told me she knew more than she showed.

My face hardened in concentration. "I wanna know the answer to my question."

Her perfectly arched brow puckered. "One thing about me, daddy, is I don't dance or talk for free."

I pulled out a roll and held it up. "You were sayin'?"

"Bankx," she answered without hesitation.

"He in here tonight?" I asked, muscles in my jaw bunched.

She dropped down between my legs and ran her hands over my

thighs. "You wanna talk about another nigga, or you wanna talk about you and me?" she asked, diverting from the subject.

"I wanna talk about what you know."

"I mind my money and my business. I ain't told you shit that you can't find on Google."

"Nah, see, you seem a lot smarter to me than that. I wanna know everything you know about this place and who runs this mothafucka," I pushed out before tossing another stack on the stage without batting an eye. "You scratch my back, and I'll scratch yours."

"Is that right?" She smirked, pupils turning into dollar signs.

"Yeah, and if I like what you sayin', there's more where that came from."

She steepled her fingers as the acrylic on her long nails clicked against each other. "Oh, yeah? Like what?"

"Ain't nothing like the feeling of cold hard cash flipping through your fingertips, right?"

She grinned like the Cheshire cat. "Mmm. You're two of my favorite things, freaky and filthy rich," she moaned before doing a backbend and spreading her legs like the peace sign over my shoulders. "What do you wanna know?"

I slid a few more bills into the side of her G-string. "We'll talk about that at the bachelor party. Until then, you just make sure that tongue of yours stays tied."

"Don't worry, daddy. I keep these lips tight. Both sets."

"Bet."

"What they call you, anyway?" she asked before giving me a once over.

I was iced out from head to toe, smiling. "The Punani Rusher like Usher," I informed her, quoting Treach from Naughty by Nature.

She smirked before bending down to collect her earnings. "That's cute or whatever."

"What's your name, beautiful?"

"Asian Bliss."

"Your *real* name."

"I'll tell you mine if you tell me yours."

I looked left and right before answering, "Baby."

"Mmm, times up, Baby," she responded as her heels clicked toward the door.

"You not gon' tell me your name?"

"Jade," she whispered in my ear before kissing my cheek.

I slid my phone out of my pocket as I made my way down the hall. After opening my messages, I sent a text to Chief and Rome.

ME:

We need to link. It's urgent.

BANKX

"The shipment will be delayed by about another twenty-four to forty-eight hours. My guys have had to take some detours due to some unforeseen traffic issues over in Houston," Reynard, my uncle, told me.

I took a puff from my blunt and paused, head momentarily trapped in a cloud of smoke. "That ain't no thing," I choked out, weed smoke sliding from my nostrils.

"Glad to hear it. How's my investment doing?"

"The club is straight. Business is boomin' like I said it would," I stated, kissing my fingertips. "This was the business venture I needed to get me back in the game and back on top, Unc."

"I'm glad I could help, nephew. It's the least I can do after you held it down behind bars for all those years. I'll never forget your loyalty."

I tilted my chin in a nod. "Real recognize real."

"But you're out now, and it's time to show the city you're back like you never left."

I scratched my beard. "Yeah."

"So, what's next in your master plan?" he inquired.

Before I could answer, I heard a knock on the door. My vision narrowed to a pinprick as I studied the security camera feed before adjusting to normal after realizing it was Jade knocking at my door.

"Yo, Unc, I gotta go handle somethin'. Let me hit you back," I reassured him before ending the call.

Not only was Reynard Shaw my blood uncle, but he was also my plug. He ran the streets of Atlanta and had connections from Miami to Houston, New York, Chicago, and back around again. Aside from the rainy-day money I had stashed offshore, he fronted me the cash to buy the old club and help fund the renovations so we could push his drugs through it when we reopened. In my eyes, it was a win for both of us. I pushed my thoughts of him to the side and hit my blunt one more time before yelling for Jade to come in.

A smile clung to her cherry-red painted lips. "Hey, you."

"Wassup?"

"You good?"

I rubbed the back of my neck. "It's nothin'. How we doin' out there tonight?"

Her shoulders rose and fell. "It's good. Could be better if these lazy bitches got off their asses more and started pressin' these niggas for dances."

"Hit up Nique at the bar. She'll get 'em right, loosen' they pockets right up.

She smirked. "Cool. Oh, and Honey Moan said she don't feel good and can't go back out there tonight. I told her you weren't gon' be too happy about that, but here I am, just the messenger. Don't shoot me," her voice trailed off.

I sucked my teeth. It was always somethin' with those bitches. "Tell her to pack her shit up and go home," I demanded as I relit my blunt.

"Aight, then."

"Oh, and one more thing. You've got an admirer," she recalled, leaning in so I could blow her a shotgun.

A line of confusion materialized between my brows before I gave in to her silent demand. "What you mean by that?"

"Somebody came through and dropped bands tryna get information on you," she informed me before exhaling smoke.

"Information on me? Who the fuck was it? A fed?"

"Nah, he ain't strike me as a fed. Said his name was Baby. Light-skinned, pretty, wavy hair, flashy pretty boy type."

From her description alone, I knew exactly who she was talking about. "Mmm," I grumbled, "what you tell 'em?"

She shrugged. "Nothin' Google couldn't."

"What else he say?"

"Something about his brother getting married. He's throwing a private party and wants me and the girls to come dance."

"When?"

"I don't know all the details right off hand, but he knows who to reach out to for setting that up. He said the wedding was in a few weeks, so it's gotta be soon."

I dipped my chin in a quick nod. I trusted her, but only to a point. She was too beautiful to be fully trusted. I knew these bitches had bills to pay and would say or do whatever to ensure that happened. Jade and a few other girls were my scouts. They were my eyes and ears around the club, and in return, I broke them off something extra whenever they came through with information. If I knew anything, it was that when there were drinks and titties in the same room, niggas lips started flapping, and the dollars started flowing quicker. I'd been laying low since I'd gotten out, but I'd never taken my eyes off the Snow brothers. I was going to wreak havoc on their family for destroying mine.

"Aight. Good work. Keep your ears and eyes open for me when you're there."

"Don't I always?"

"I wanna know that nigga's every move."

"Who is he anyway?"

"A dead man walkin'. Him and his fuckin' brothers."

"Damn, B. What did he do to you?"

I slowly turned my head to her. "I've been good to you since you've known me?" I asked, more of a comment than a question.

"Of course you have."

"Good, because there's something I want you to do for me. There will be a big payday at the end of it for you."

"How much we talkin'?"

"Fifty stacks."

Her eyes widened. "What you need me to do?"

"I gotta know you ain't gon' be scared."

She frowned. "Scared? I ain't scared of a mothafuckin' thing, especially no man that bleeds like I do," she confirmed.

I smirked. "Bet. Make sure the door is locked. We got some shit to discuss."

I STEPPED OUT OF THE HOSPITAL ON MY LUNCH BREAK, WAVING AT Norman, the security guard, with a smile across my face as I flashed him my badge. I was a second-year surgical resident at the University of Miami Health System. We'd become well acquainted with each other because I would always lose or misplace my badge at the worst possible times when I was an intern. As I'd gotten halfway down the sidewalk, my phone began vibrating in my scrub pocket. I pulled it out to see a photo of my best friend, Jade, and me with her name across the screen.

"Waddup, bitch," I answered her FaceTime call with a dimpled smile.

"Ain't shit, hoe. You know what time it is. Where your mothafuckin' lunch at?" she snapped, her perfectly arched eyebrows in disarray.

"About that...does this count?" I asked as I pulled a Chewy bar and a Capri Sun out of my lab coat pocket and held it up to the screen.

"How fuckin old are you, Skai?"

I smacked my lips and rolled my cocoa-brown eyes

simultaneously. "Whatever! If it's one thing about me, I'ma drink a mothafuckin' Capri Sun, aight?"

"Okay, DOCTOR Daniels. You do you, boo."

"How's your day been?" I asked her before puncturing the silver pouch with a straw.

"It's been chill. You know me; I do nails at Ba's shop during the day and dance at the club at night."

I smacked my lips again. "I still don't understand why you dropped out of med school, Jade. You were easily the smartest in our class."

"I know I went against the grain, but as much as Ba and my mother wanted me to become some hotshot doctor, it just wasn't in me. I can't say I ever saw myself making a living on the pole, but I'm booked and I'm busy, bitch. I make in one night what most of these Miami bitches make in six months. Your girl is fulfilled, aight? So don't worry about me. You worry about yourself and them student loans. Med school ain't cheap."

"Sho ain't." I sighed while rolling my eyes to the sky. "Shit, sometimes I wish I was up there on that pole with you. Especially whenever I have to do a fuckin' rectal exam."

"Yeah, no. I do *not* miss that shit at all, and when I say shit, I do mean literal shit." She snickered.

The two of us shared a wide mouth laugh. She and I had been thick as thieves since our first day of med school. We instantly bonded over being biracial and losing our mothers at young ages, mine from a brain tumor when I was thirteen and hers from a car accident when she was only six. She'd been working at her father's nail shop to help him make ends meet since she was twelve. After her mother passed, her father, or Ba, as she called him, fully immersed her in the Vietnamese culture, aiming to starve off the other half of her that made her who she was, a Vietnamese and Black woman. I'd only met him a sprinkle of times, but from what I gathered, he was a proud Vietnamese man who always pushed Jade to be the best. In his eyes, that meant becoming a doctor. To her, that meant doing what she loved, dancing. When our third year rolled around, it was almost as if a switch flipped inside her. She no longer cared to hold in how much she hated the direction her life was going in and told me she'd decided to drop out to pursue dance full-time. Of course, I tried to reason with her and change her mind, but the decision had been made. Within a matter of months, she fully immersed herself in everything her father tried to steer her away from. Soon, her tawny skin had become inked with so many tattoos you could barely find an un-inked piece of flesh. I was admittedly nervous when she admitted to me that she'd started secretly dancing at a few clubs across the city, but over the years, the pole kept her pretty and paid, so I couldn't complain. She was my girl, and I was going to hold her down regardless; it didn't matter if she had the abbreviation of doctor in front of her name or not. I didn't trust many, but I trusted Jade with my life. With my crazy work schedule at the hospital and her working two jobs, we'd resorted to weekly FaceTime lunch dates to fill the void.

"Anyway, bitch. I got news!" Jade chirped.

"Listening," I answered in mid chew.

"I met some nigga at the club over the weekend. He was dropping bands or whatever, then said he wanted to host a private party because his brother was getting married. I tell him it's ten bands up front for six bitches, plus tips, and the nigga didn't even bat one of his long, pretty ass eyelashes. I'm like, okay, let me let you go holla at the bitch who takes care of all that. And why I just got a text with all the logistics. Like, he finna make it rain, sleet, and snow this weekend."

"Congrats! Sounds like an easy payday."

"Exactly! You should tag along."

"Me? Bitch, I ain't no stripper!"

"Trust me; I've seen your moves. We know your stiff-back ass is too uptight to flow around the pole."

"Shut up! I do not have a stiff back!"

"You know that meme with the girl from Bob's Burgers twerking? That's exactly what you look like." She cackled.

I smacked my lips. "You know what, fuck you!"

"You can't help that you're half-white, Skai. No rhythm comes with the territory."

"I'm about to hang up on your ass!"

"Okay, chill. I was just joking. But for real, you should come."

"I am off this weekend, but I think I'll pass on this one."

"What do you mean you'll pass? You know damn well you have nothin' better to do."

I swung my head in a no. "Drug dealers ain't my thing, that's all."

"There you go! Who said anything about drug dealers? I just said the man was paid! And so what if he is slanging? You gotta know your way around these niggas pockets, girl."

I gave a dismissive shrug of my shoulders. "I guess."

"Besides, I like me a roughneck. The kitty only gets wet for niggas with street status these days anyway."

I snickered at her comment. "You're a mess; you know that?"

"And so are you, Skai! You wanna know what your problem is?"

"What's my problem, Jade?" I quizzed sarcastically while rolling my eyes skyward.

"You think too damn hard and too damn much," she spat.

"I'm a doctor, Jade. Am I not supposed to use my brain?"

"You know what the fuck I mean! Just let loose for once! What's the harm? It's one night!"

"You're going to be working. I'll stick out like a sore thumb," I whined.

"You'll be fine. There will be so many bitches in there; they ain't gon' notice one more."

"They will if I'm not dancing," I countered.

She smacked her lips. "All I hear is excuses."

"I should probably just stay in and rest up. I'm so tired that 'let's take a nap together' is my official love language right now."

"Again, excuses."

"Ugh," I groaned while turning in the direction of the hospital before quickly jerking back around. "Shit!"

"What is it?" Jade quizzed, voice heightened with concern.

A quick no jerked my head, attempting to put her suspicions to rest. "Nothing. It's nothing."

"All that loud ass shuffling and moving you doing over there sure says otherwise."

I groaned. "Ugh, it's Malik."

Dr. Malik Harrison was an anesthesiologist fellow that I'd dated for six months if I could even call it dating. It was more like a situationship with benefits. Things were good up until two weeks ago when I stumbled across an engagement ring with the words "N and M Forever" inscribed inside the platinum band after having mind-blowing sex in his condo. Clearly, he'd had other commitments that had nothing to do with me. I didn't even bother to confront him about it or ask why. Instead, I vowed never to date or *fuck* someone I worked with *ever* again. I'd been ducking and dodging him ever since. Pretty, light-skinned niggas were my kryptonite; always had been. Malik was tall, had amazingly baby-smooth caramel skin, and a smile that could change a bitch life. On top of all that danger, he had the thickest dick and most opulent stroke game I'd ever encountered. Just thinking about that missile swinging between his legs made my knees turn to water.

"Oh, boo We hate Malik," Jade jeered, jarring me back to the present.

"Shit, do you think he saw me?"

"Hey, Skai!" he called out from twenty feet away.

"Damn, he clocked yo' ass fast as shit. I'ma let you handle that."

"No! Your ass better stay on the phone with me!" I demanded before quickly placing my AirPods into my ears so he wouldn't catch wind of our conversation.

"See! This shit right here is exactly why you should come outside and play this weekend, Skai! It's smelling real single outside!"

"Shut up!"

"Think about it, aight? You're so uptight all the time, Skai. It's time you let loose for just a second."

Before I had the opportunity to respond how I wanted to, Malik closed in on me, and I blurted out the first shit that came to mind. "Mmhm. Oh no! That's so bad. Is there anything I can do?" I asked Jade, loud and suspect as hell.

Malik stepped up to me with a serious look across his caramel face and my eyes darted directly to his lips. He had the kind of mouth that was made for kissing. "Skai, can I talk to you for a second?"

"Can it wait? I'm, uh, in the middle of something right now. Family drama!"

"Oh, um—I was hoping that we could t–"

"Okay, thanks, bye," I mumbled over my shoulder to him before zooming off.

Back inside, I headed up to the fourth floor, excited to be scrubbing in on a laparotomy. All the excitement instantly drained from my body the minute I checked the board to see that Malik, the *one* person I'd been trying my hardest to dodge, had been listed as the anesthesiologist assisting during the surgery. As hard as I'd been working to keep us apart, the universe had made it clear that it had other plans.

"Fuck," I grumbled through my mask.

Sometimes I couldn't believe that I was already a resident. Like, I'd survived med school and my intern year. Somehow med school felt like an eternity ago and like yesterday at the same time. My parents weren't famous surgeons. Medicine and healthcare didn't run in my family. It wasn't until my mother's diagnosis that I became interested in medicine. For months, I witnessed her struggle with crippling headaches and migraines, and even a couple of seizures. One day while we were standing in the middle of the cereal aisle, she dropped the box of Cinnamon Toast Crunch to the floor and told me she couldn't see, that her vision had suddenly gone blurry, and that I needed to call my dad.

We rushed her to the hospital, and after the doctors ran multiple tests, they discovered that she had glioblastoma, an aggressive brain tumor that had been snowballing over time. I watched her fight her way through standard therapy treatments to extend the eighteen months the doctors gave her to live. We all knew no matter how many surgeries or rounds of chemo and radiation she put herself through, there wasn't a cure. She passed twelve and a half months later with both of us by her side. Since then, I knew medicine was what I wanted to pursue. I wanted to find a cure so no family would have to go through what mine did.

"Some surgery, huh?" Malik inquired as we scrubbed our hands at the sink four hours later.

I nodded without so much as a glance up at him. "Yup."

"You did great in there."

His compliment disarmed me, causing me to look up just in time for his dimpled smile and bone-white teeth to annihilate me. "Um, thanks."

I turned to walk away, heading for my locker to go home for the evening. All I wanted to do was grab my shit so I could get home, take a shower, and crash. After coming off a twenty-two-and-a-half-hour shift, my zombie-like fingers slowly reached up to tap the elevator button. Before the doors could fully close, I saw a melanated hand slice between them before Malik showed up inside.

"Hey," he called out.

"Hi," I mumbled.

It was almost as if God wanted me to fuck that man. Why else would he keep dangling him in front of me like that?

"Heading out?"

My tired eyes darted down at my purse hanging over my left shoulder and then back at him as if to say, *duh, what does it look like,* although none of those words escaped my lips. "Mmhm," I uttered with a quick dip of my chin.

The two of us stood awkwardly on opposite sides of the elevator before he blurted out an aggravated "Fuck this."

My forehead creased at the sound of his voice. "What?"

He reached out and pressed the emergency stop button before turning to me. "Skai, we need to talk."

I disagreed. "No, we don't."

"Bullshit. I've missed us, and I know you have, too," he admitted while gently swiping a loose curl dangling in the center of my forehead.

"There is no us," I confirmed before swatting his hand away and flinging the hair back from my brow. I didn't need him fixing me.

"Don't be like that. Besides, if anyone should be mad, it's me."

"How do you figure that?" I quizzed, arms folded tightly across my chest.

"Because you're the one that ghosted me!"

My blood began to boil. "That's because I'm above fucking married men or men that are about to become engaged! That's right, Malik. I found the ring in your apartment! That's why I left!"

His dark brows rose with surprise and then furrowed. "Why in the hell didn't you just tell me that?"

"So now I'm the only one that's required to be honest in this relationship, or whatever the fuck this is? All you had to do was tell me Nichelle was back in the picture. But I guess you're just the type who's gotta have his cake and another cake too."

Nichelle was Malik's on-again-off-again "girlfriend." They'd been in each other's lives for six and a half years. He was her first. Thus, he felt some deeper connection to her that I refused to understand. Over the years, she'd dished out hall pass after hall pass so that he could run off and fulfill his sexual desires without the added shame or guilt. As long as he didn't bring her back any diseases or illegitimate babies, he got to do whatever and *whoever* he wanted, and she got to keep her man. I didn't understand why she continuously handed herself the short end of the deal, but to some women, having half of a man was better than not having one at all. Six months ago, when we started messing around, he told me they'd officially ended things. She'd gotten accepted as a fellow at Johns Hopkins in Baltimore, and he was here in Miami. In love or not, he wasn't down for the distance when he could be dicking down bitches who weren't over a thousand miles away.

"Listen, Skai—I was gonna talk to you about it, okay? I swear I was."

"When? At your engagement party? Bachelor party? I mean, be for real, Malik. You at least owe me that!"

He let out a frustrated sigh. "You're right. Our shit is complicated, okay? You've always known that."

I scoffed. "All relationships are complicated, Malik. If they weren't, everyone would be in one."

I could hear the lies so clearly now. I must've been too distracted by the D or something. He lowered his head in defeat and shot his sympathetic, pretty brown eyes at me.

"I meant what I said. I do miss us, Skai."

"What's the point of missing something you never wanted in the first place?"

He narrowed the six-foot gap between us and let his fingertips cling to my scrub-clad waist. "Stop. Malik, stop."

"We both know you don't want me to do that," he mumbled against my lips.

I sighed, weakening by the second as he seduced me with his eyes. His shiny white teeth glistened whenever he opened his mouth to speak. "I have pre-rounds at six in the morning."

He brushed my hair away from my neck and gently nibbled on it. My heart began to beat more rapidly.

"I need a shower, Malik."

He remained silent, allowing his hands to roam freely over my breasts, hips, and ass.

"Malik, I'm exhausted."

I knew rolling around on top of him meant a full twenty-four-hour, caffeine-fueled shift, but that didn't stop his advances, and I was fresh out of excuses. Somewhere between him hitting the elevator button to get us moving again and the doors sliding open as his hand crept up my thigh, we ended up in the sixty-nine position on the bottom bunk in the nearest on-call room. Forty-five minutes later, I slid outside the on-call room after backsliding with Malik while fully knowing he was engaged or planning to be engaged. Was I proud of my actions? Not in the least. That shame intensified when I realized I'd put my scrub top back on inside out. I never wanted to unfuck someone so bad in my life. Feeling defeated and in need of a release, I pulled out my phone to text Jade as I trekked down the long corridor and outside to my car.

ME:

About that party... I'm in.

Saturday night rolled around, and I was excited to let my hair down for once, literally and figuratively. At work, I always wore my hair in a top knot bun or pulled it back into a low ponytail. I usually preferred to wear my hair curly, but for the sake of stepping out, I blew out my natural curls and tossed in some beach waves. From the hallway bathroom, I heard a key jingling in the lock and knew it was Jade letting herself into my apartment.

"Hoodie hoo!" she called out.

"In the bathroom," I replied.

"Hey!"

"Hey! You look cute," I praised, admiring her sparkling mini-dress and heels.

"Thanks. I'll change once we get to the party. I at least wanna walk in that bitch lookin' classy before I start pussy poppin' for dollars," she sneered.

"Yeah, okay. Don't forget to put my spare key back!" I demanded.

"Yeah, yeah. Maybe you wouldn't be so pressed about me putting it back if you didn't lose your keys so much," she quipped.

"Why are you ridin' me already, huh? I'm just trying to have a good time tonight."

"And a good time you shall have, girl. I can almost promise you that. What are you wearing?"

"Options are laid out on the bed. You know what to do."

"Thank you."

Of course, Jade picked out the shortest, strappiest, tightest one. When she'd finished dressing me, I was clad in a strappy black mini-dress with a pair of clear heels that laced up to my calves. After putting on some gold accessories and swooping my head full of jet-black curls over to the right side of my face, I deemed myself ready.

I sat in the passenger seat of Jade's Mercedes coupe, letting the warm wind tussle my curls. I shifted uncomfortably against her leather interior, trying to unstick my bare thighs from the seat.

"When we go in here tonight, just act cool, aight?" Jade reminded me.

"How else am I supposed to act?"

"I mean, don't be your awkward ass, straight and narrow self. Just relax. Here, hit this shit one time," she offered, passing her blunt my way.

I wagged my head. "No thanks. You know I can't do that shit."

She smacked her lips. "One hit ain't gon' kill you. Plus, don't act all brand new like you ain't been high before. I was there with you in med school. I know the stories."

I rolled my eyes. "Whatever. It was a stressful time in my life, okay? I'm above all that now."

"Suit yourself, friend. You gon' need somethin' to loosen you up, though, or these niggas gon' eat your pretty ass alive."

"What do you mean? I thought you said I was just gonna be able to blend in."

"And you will, as long as you get that face of yours together."

I winced. "What's wrong with my face."

"You tell me. You the one sittin' over there lookin' stuck on stupid."

"I slept with Malik," I confessed with ease.

"And?"

K.L. Hall

"And, you know I'm trying to quit him. But his dick just keeps pullin' me back," I whined.

"Girl, how many times and how many ways do we need to say fuck his triflin' ass? That nigga needs to know it's a privilege to be fucking with you, okay? That's all I'm saying."

I sighed. "You're right, I know."

"Shit, that's exactly why I be lying to niggas. I mean, why not? They lie and use us all the time!"

"You're right about that," I mumbled while silently reflecting on all my past failed relationships with fuck boys.

"I'm on my Lori Harvey shit, okay? And fuck any mothafucka who got somethin' to say about it. They can suck my ass through a straw!"

"Maybe I need to be on that same vibe."

"Come on over, Skai. The weather is nice."

I giggled. "Hush."

"All I'm sayin' is, you gotta know your way around these niggas' pockets, girl. Leave all that love and feelings shit out of it. And trust, what one won't give you, another will."

Instead of responding, I leaned my head against the headrest and let her words sink in. I hadn't fully decided if I agreed with them or not, but I couldn't deny the game she was spitting. Jade had always been a hustler, a smart-ass one at that. She had it all; beauty and was both book and street-smart.

The elevator door opened to the penthouse, and my nose was immediately greeted by the pungent aroma of marijuana, sex, and crisp dollar bills hanging in the air. I stepped out behind Jade, and a woman dressed in black lingerie handed us two different masquerade masks. Relieved that I could blend in a bit easier, I quickly slid it over my eyes. With my identity hidden, I relaxed and scanned the large penthouse with floor-to-ceiling windows that provided a panoramic view of the city. The music was blasting so loud that I swore I felt the marble floor vibrating beneath us. The space was filled with minimal, modern decor. A bar was set up in the open kitchen area, a DJ booth overlooked the second level, and three chrome poles in the middle of the living floor as the main attraction for the occasion.

"I'm about to find the other girls and go change. You good?"

"Yeah."

"Cool. Get a drink at the bar and loosen up. There are plenty of people in here. No one is going to notice you unless you want them to. Who knows, you might even leave with a stack," she quipped with a wink.

"Go handle your business. I'll be fine," I assured her.

I made my way through the sea of people and over to the bar to get a glass of champagne with a sliced strawberry floating at the bottom of my flute. While taking a sip, I continued to scan the party. In every direction I turned, there seemed to be a new pair of titties and ass bouncing around. A half-naked woman was riding a mechanical bull in the middle of a ball pit to my left, and a group of masked men—each with their personal champagne bottles glued to their hands like baseball gloves—were cheering her on. One was making his way around the party, shooting dollar bills from a money gun. When Jade came out and took to the center pole, everything seemed to pause. Over the years, I'd seen her dance probably a hundred times, but I never got over watching people's reactions to seeing her for the first time. They were always in awe. A smile tugged at my lips when the money started to cover the floor around her. She was in her element and doing precisely what she'd come there to do; get paid.

I spotted the exit to the balcony and decided to head out for some fresh air. After downing the remaining gulp of champagne in my glass, I rested my elbows against the balcony railing and pulled out my phone to see a text from Malik. My heart somersaulted in my chest before I opened it to see a dick pic followed by the purple demon emoji. I sucked my teeth.

"This mothafucka can't be serious," I mumbled before swiping to delete our entire text thread. He was a sinking ship, and it was past time that I learned how to swim.

"What nigga put that sour look on your face?" a male voice spoke up.

"Excuse me?" I snapped, twisting my neck in the direction of a masked man. The same one I'd witnessed shooting dollars out of a money gun inside. I had been standing there so deep in thought that I didn't notice I was no longer outside alone.

"You heard me. Gotta be a nigga on your mind if you ain't worried about all the money flowin' around inside."

I huffed. "Yeah, well, you got me there."

"Wasn't hard. There are too many females here, and you are the only one who doesn't seem concerned about making any money tonight. What, you ain't got no bills to pay?"

I twisted my lips. "Trust me, I've got plenty, but I'm not a stripper."

"Then what are you?"

"A doctor," I asserted.

"Word?"

"Yeah, *word*," I mocked him.

"So, if a nigga out here fuckin' around in these streets and get a bullet put in me, you can handle that, right?"

"Uh, yes. But please don't do that. I've seen my share of gunshot wounds, and they are never pretty."

He ran his hand down the wavy, black goatee. "I got you. That's wassup, though. For what it's worth, I think scrubs are sexy."

His confession caused me to belt out a laugh. It wasn't because it was uncanny but because it was something I'd heard so often.

"I like your laugh."

"Thanks."

"Bet you got a beautiful face to match."

"Maybe I do."

"I'll show you mine if you show me yours," he reasoned, toying with his mask. I gave a soft chuckle before pulling the mask away from my eyes. "Damn."

A wrinkle cut across my forehead. "What?"

He let his gaze wander slowly down my body. "You're fuckin' gorgeous."

I felt my cheeks turning crimson red. "Oh, um, thank you. Guess it's your turn."

He removed his mask, and I instantly clenched my thighs. His smooth skin was the shade of desert sand that had been kissed by the sun. He had big, cocoa-brown eyes with long eyelashes that naturally curled skyward. His head, full of soft, jet-black coils, was pulled back into a ponytail that landed at the nape of his neck, and he had a few loose curls dangling over his fresh edge-up. From the thin mustache sitting over his lips to the big, square diamonds dancing in his ears. He honestly was fucking gorgeous.

"Damn, a nigga must be ugly."

I chuckled, trying my darndest not to start salivating at the sight of his juicy brown lips. "I'm so sorry. No, of course, you're uh, you're gorgeous too!" I laughed harder.

"What's your name, gorgeous?"

"Skai. You?"

"Judah, but everyone calls me Baby."

"Why, Baby?" I wondered if it had anything to do with his skin's smoothness.

"I'm the youngest of three boys."

Suddenly, it clicked. He was the baller that Jade told me about. "Ah, the brother of the bachelor?"

"Yeah. I'm hosting tonight. You enjoying yourself?"

"The champagne was good, so sure. You?"

"I am. I only came out here to breathe a bit. It's a mah'fuckin' jungle in there."

I dipped my chin in a nod. "You're right about that," I answered, thankful we didn't have to yell over the music to hear each other.

"How long you been saving lives and shit?" he inquired.

Before I could answer, another man came outside. "There you are. I've been lookin' all over for your ass. I gotta holla at you real quick."

Baby looked at me. "Don't move," he insisted, "I wanna finish this."

I nodded. "Sure."

He stepped off with the man while I glanced down at the time on my phone. Somehow almost an hour had flown by. Although I'd enjoyed my conversation with Baby, it was getting late, and I was ready to go home. After waiting ten minutes for Baby to come back, I decided to call myself an Uber and find Jade to let her know I was calling it a night.

I made my way back inside, dead set on locating Jade. When I finally found her, she was down the hallway with her ear cupped to the door, ear hustling on the conversation behind a door that wasn't fully closed before pulling out her phone to snap a few quick pictures and text someone.

"Jade, what are you doing?" I asked, walking up to her.

She quickly put her phone down. "Nothing, come on," she insisted, grabbing me by the arm.

We hurried back down the hall. "What was that all about? What were you doing back there?" I asked her.

"Nothing, don't worry about it. What's up? You good?"

"I'm fine. I was just coming to find you to let you know I'm about to go."

"Go? Why are you leaving so early?"

"It's almost two o'clock in the morning, Jade. Plus, my Uber is outside."

"Fine, okay. You sure you good?"

"I'm good. Are *you* good?"

"Yeah, I am," she persisted before tearing her eyes down at her phone, "text me when you get home, aight?"

"Yeah, okay. You be safe."

She pulled me into a quick hug. "I'm always safe, Skai."

BABY

I TORE THROUGH THE CROWD, DRUNK AND A LITTLE MORE DISORIENTED than I intended, eager to get back to the balcony to finish talking to Skai. By the time I got out there, she was gone. I turned around and was immediately met by Asian Bliss.

"You lookin' for me?" she inquired before letting her chest brush up against mine.

I glanced down at her, and I lost my train of thought for a split second. "Nah, but I found you."

"Are my girls showing you a good time?"

"Yeah. It's lit. I was lookin' for somebody in particular, though. I think she said her name was Skai."

Her brows arched in surprise. "Nah, I don't know nobody named Skai. But don't you worry about that. I'm sure I can find you just what you need."

She slipped her hand in mine and parted the crowd until we landed at the heels of a mocha-skinned goddess with long, black hair that swayed against the tip of her ass crack. A smile ran around her lips, and I smiled back.

"You like what you see?"

I bobbed my head. "Mmhm."

"This my girl, Diamond Pu$$y. Diamond, this is one of the groomsmen, and he's the host for tonight's festivities. I think we should give him a little parting gift for being so generous to us tonight, don't you?"

She cheesed before stepping away from the pole and draping her long, chocolate arms over my shoulders. "I think that sounds real nice."

I don't know why I expected her to sound like a city girl, but she had a strong Jamaican accent that made my dick jump in my pants. "What do you ladies have in mind?"

"Mmm, I've got a lot of things on this mind, daddy. But I don't know if you can handle the both of us," Asian Bliss purred before gently swiping her long, acrylic nail down my cheek.

"Trust I can handle anything you throw at me."

"You standin' on that?" Diamond Pu$$y asked.

I dipped my chin in a nod. "Ten toes down, sexy. All you gotta do is say the word, and we can be out."

They turned to each other and smiled. "Let me go get our things, and then we'll be ready to go," Asian Bliss responded. "Diamond, why don't you go get us a few drinks for the road? I'll be right back."

A few minutes later, she met Diamond and me at the bar, and the three of us downed a round of tequila shots before heading to the elevator doors. We stumbled inside the metal box with my arms hung over their shoulders.

"Damn, I'm lit," I confessed.

"Too lit to fuck?" Asian Bliss asked.

"Never that."

"Good," Diamond added before running her hand over my dick.

When we got outside, I felt around in my pockets for my keys before Asian Bliss slipped them out of my hand. "Let me drive."

I swung my head from left to right. "I–I can drive."

"Nah, you're too saucy, daddy. You'll fuck around and kill us all. I got it. What's your address?"

"My address? Let's just, let's just go–go and get a room some– somewhere," I insisted, slurring every other word.

"He sounds like he's stalling," Diamond inserted.

"Ain't nobody stalling."

"Then what's your address, daddy? Here, just type it in my phone. I promise we don't bite."

"Hmph, speak for yourself," Diamond sassed with a smirk.

Head spinning, I looked at them both. I didn't make a habit of bringing bitches back to the crib, but they were both ready and willing, so I didn't bother putting too much thought into it. I swiped the phone out of her hand and quickly plugged in my address. She tapped the key fob to unlock the doors and got into the front seat while Diamond lured me to the back.

"So, you tryna get this party started or what?"

"What do you have in mind?"

"Pass me that blunt up there in the visor."

Asian Bliss put my blunt to her lips and hit it a few times while she lit it. She then passed it back to Diamond, who blew a shotgun to me. "Damn, this that good shit," she complimented.

"Only the best everything around me."

Before I knew it, the three of us were zooming down the highway on the way to my crib. Somewhere along the way, Diamond managed to wrap her juicy lips around my dick and started giving me top in the backseat.

"Mmm shit," I growled, pushing her mouth down deeper as my eyes rolled to the back of my head.

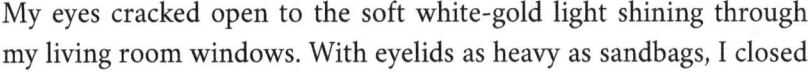

My eyes cracked open to the soft white-gold light shining through my living room windows. With eyelids as heavy as sandbags, I closed them again to block out the brightness until I could come out of my semiconscious state. After fully waking, my limbs expanded slowly until I hit a large mass. My eyes crossed, then refocused on the couch.

"Shit," I groaned.

As badly as I wanted to get off the floor and get my shit together, my body was too heavy, and my skull was thumping like an 808. Unable to greet the sunlight or coordinate effective movement, I closed my eyes again and allowed my brain to replay the last few scenes of my night in hopes it could help unjumble my fuckin' thoughts.

I remembered the three of us got back to the crib and drank, kissed, and touched some more before shit started to get fuzzy, and I started zoning in and out. Even with my eyes closed, the last thing I recalled hearing before I blacked out was them talking around me while I lay slumped against the couch.

"This nigga dick is too big for me to keep sucking it like this."

"Since when your ass don't like a challenge?"

"I'm just sayin', are you sure it's here?"

"I heard him talkin' to his brothers about a stash. Just give me some time to find it!"

My eyes shot open again, and for the first time, everything was fixed and focused. I slowly began to pull myself off the ground with a carousel of thoughts in my head as I stumbled down the hallway. My legs didn't stop until I was standing in front of my safe with the door cracked wide open.

"They got me. Them bitches fuckin' got me," I growled, staring down at the empty safe.

I staggered back down the hallway in search of my phone. I needed to speak to Rome and Chief immediately. All I could do was hope they were both in a sounder place of mind than I was. Even after shedding the sleep from my brain, I knew those hoes drugged me because of how sluggish I felt.

Forty-five minutes later, my brothers were at my door with frowns on their mugs.

"What the fuck happened?" Chief raged.

"Those bitches drugged me and robbed me."

"What bitches? From the party last night?"

I nodded before guzzling down a bottle of water. "Yeah."

"How bad is it? What all did they get?" Rome asked.

"Those hoes cracked my safe and took everything in it."

Chief's eyebrow lifted in question. "What the fuck was in it?"

I clenched my jaw, almost unwilling to open my mouth at all. "Two-hundred and fifty stacks…."

Rome frowned. "And that's all?"

I shot my eyes over at Rome and then Chief. "Well, is it?" he asked.

"Nah."

"Nigga, stop with the suspenseful shit and tell us what the fuck they got up off your ass!" Chief demanded.

I parted my lips to answer, knowing the two words that were about to fall off my lips would send them both into a frenzy. "The diamonds."

I watched both sets of their eyes widen. "What the fuck did you just say?" Rome asked, face screwed into a beastly frown.

"You heard me, nigga," I answered him.

"God damnit, Baby," Chief muttered before expelling a long sigh. "I swear to God, your stupid ass never misses a chance to fuck somethin' up, do you? How the fuck did you let this happen, huh?"

"And how the fuck did they get inside your safe in the first place? Did you tell them the code?" Rome inquired.

Chief grumbled. "Or did you make it easy and leave it sittin' wide open for them hoes?"

I sucked my teeth while cutting my eyes at them. "I know it's bad, aight? I was fuckin' targeted! What do you want me to fuckin' do about it now?"

"I want you to stop makin' such dumb ass decisions, Baby. Yeah, you young, and we let you wild out, but you gotta grow the fuck up, lil' nigga and soon! I'm tired of cleanin' up your fuckin' messes," Chief lectured.

I slammed my eyes shut and laid my head in my hands. No sooner than that, another flashback from the night before popped into my head.

"What did he say the code was again? Two, Seven, eleven?"

"Shit. I thought he said Two, seventeen, four. This mothafucka is slurring and shit. Just gimme a minute, aight? Keep 'em occupied."

"Bitch, the floor got 'em occupied. He's face down, and I ain't heard him make a sound in a minute, so he probably fucked around and passed out."

"Good, come and help me with this shit."

I snapped back into the present in an uproar. "Just shut the fuck up about it, aight? You ain't my fuckin' father, nigga! I'm grown enough to handle this shit. Trust and believe I'ma find them bitches!" I hissed.

"Those bitches should be the least of your worries right now."

Creases flocked together on my forehead. "What the fuck you mean?"

Chief sucked his teeth. "See, your response proves you still playin' checkers when you should be playing chess, Baby. But, you grown, then handle this shit on your own."

"Oh, so it's all on me now? All on my shoulders?"

"You fuckin' right it is! I don't need this shit right before my fuckin' wedding, nigga!" Chief screamed, veins throbbing at his temple.

My eyebrows jogged up to my forehead. "Nigga, all you've ever been worried about is yourself! My shit got hit! I'm the one with the target on my mothafuckin' back, and all you can talk about is you! You a selfish mothafucka, and you always have been, Chief!"

Rome interjected. "Look, the damage is done now, aight? A target on my back is a target on us all. Both of you mothafuckas know that!" his voice boomed. "The truth is, them bitches caught you with your pants down and fucked you, Baby. Now, what the fuck are we gon' do about it?"

"I already told you I'ma pay them hoes a visit."

He shook his head. "Ain't no need when you already know who was behind this shit! Think about it, Baby, we already know that nigga Bankx runs the club those bitches work at."

Chief grunted. "Bitches were probably a scout from the beginning, and you led the snakes right into our grass."

"If they turn the diamonds over to him, then we already know we gon' have a bigger war on our hands. You niggas ready for that?" Rome asked, eyeing Chief and me.

"I'm ready for whatever, whenever," I assured them.

"*La Familia* over everything, right?" Chief added.

BANKX

"IS THIS EVERYTHING YOU FOUND IN THAT NIGGA'S SAFE?" I ASKED AS I shook the contents of the bag out onto the table for the three of us to see.

Although I was pleased to be sifting through stacks of crisp, green money, I was disappointed it was all they recovered.

"Yeah, that's it," AB answered.

Unable to completely veil my anger, I sighed with a frown before swiping up stacks to give the ladies their cuts for the job. "Aight. Here's a stack for you, Diamond, and two for you, AB."

Diamond sucked her teeth. "Why is her cut bigger than mine when I'm the one doing the *real* work?" she questioned, arms folded tightly across her DD chest.

"Because I'm smarter than you," AB hissed back.

"Yo, chill. Is there a problem with how I paid you, Diamond?"

She stood still, silently cutting her eyes at the both of us. "Nah, we're good."

"Good. Diamond, you're dismissed. AB, let me holla at you real quick."

Once the door closed behind Diamond, I turned my attention to AB, giving her a once-over. She was a beautiful woman with a good head on her shoulders.

"What's up?" AB inquired, propping herself up on the edge of my desk.

"How'd tonight go?"

"I told you on the phone on our way over here it went good. He was out cold when we left."

"And you didn't run into any issues?" I questioned with a raised eyebrow.

"None. We got him lit, and Diamond did her thing to keep him occupied while I worked on his safe. It was right where you said it would be. How'd you know where to find it?"

"Call it a calculated guess," I answered with a lazy shrug.

The bitch didn't need to know that this was more personal than business. I knew that mothafucka too well. When we used to do business together, he always kept his valuables in his safe in the back of his closet. A lot of years passed, but some shit never changed.

My eyes narrowed. "You ain't see no product when you were there?"

"I didn't know I was looking for product," she replied, fiddling with the diamond-studded earring in her right ear.

"You weren't. I just wanted to know."

"I ain't see no product, Bankx."

"And you sure you grabbed everything inside that safe?"

Although her body was angled toward the door, she made sure to look me square in the eyes before dipping her chin. "Yeah, I'm sure."

"You wouldn't lie to me, right?"

She placed her hands on her narrow hips. "Why would I ever have a reason to lie to you?"

I cocked my head to the side, noticing she'd answered my question with one of her own. "I'm just checking."

K.L. Hall

With a brow wrinkled, she folded her arms across her chest. "Were you looking for something in particular?"

"Nah."

Her voice rang with anticipation and hope, "So ain't nothin' I need to be on the lookout for on the next job?"

AB was a hungry mothafucka; wasn't any doubt about that shit. It was one of the things I liked about her the most. As beautiful as she was to look at and as helpful as she'd been to me, I had to put her loyalty to the test.

My head shook from side to side. "Nah. You good."

"Cool, well, it's mad late, so if you don't need anything else, I'ma go get some sleep. I gotta do nails at Ba's shop later."

"Ba? That's your father, right?"

She shot me a slight nod. "Yeah."

"Mmm," I grumbled, folding my hands together.

"What?"

I turned my half-empty glass of cognac up to my lips. "I ever tell you I killed my father when I was fourteen?" I stated it more as a comment than a question.

Her eyes widened for a split second, then returned to normal. "What he do?" she asked in a calm tone.

"He molested my sister."

She cast her eyes up to mine before parting her lips, "Then he deserved it."

Her tone was so chilling it brought a smile to my face. "I know."

"Why you tellin' me this?"

"Because I don't forgive people who cross me or fuck with things I care about."

"You shouldn't," she replied without batting one of her long eyelashes.

"Even if it's someone I care about. You know I care about you, right?"

"Yeah," she answered behind a forced smile, "I do."

"Good. Don't forget it. Good work tonight, AB. You can go."

She stood frozen in her step for a few seconds, mentally processing the test I'd put her through, not knowing whether she passed or failed. "Y–yeah. Thanks. Goodnight."

SKAI

I SHOT UP TO THE SOUND OF DOORS SLAMMING AND LIGHTS FLICKING ON
and off throughout my apartment. My heart thudded as I reached for
the aluminum baseball bat I kept beside my nightstand. I was too
chicken-shit to have any *real* defense in my possession if there were an
intruder in my apartment. Shoulders tensed, I inched for the door,
ready to swing for my life if it came down to it. When the door swung
open, a hand of fear clutched at my chest before I realized it was Jade
who was zooming around my apartment, closing all the curtains and
ensuring the windows and front door were secured as if someone
unwanted was hot on her heels.

"Jade?" I asked, clenching my chest.

"Yeah," she confirmed, "sorry I scared you."

I let out a sigh of relief. "Oh, thank God! What the hell are you
doing here so late and making all this noise?" I quizzed, setting the bat
down by the doorway.

Dressed in all black with her hair pulled into a high bun, Jade
continued to pace back and forth down the hallway, wearing a hole in
the floor and paying my question no mind.

"Jade! Will you stop moving and tell me what the hell is going on?" I demanded before groggily reaching out to place my hands on her shoulders. "Jade, you're shaking."

She looked into my eyes, and I saw nothing but fear staring back at me. "It's bad, Skai."

My brows were downturned. "What's bad?"

"Everything."

"Jade, I'm not fully awake yet, and you're acting really weird and paranoid right now, and it's scaring me. What the hell is going on? What are you talking about right now?"

"I think I fucked up, Skai. Like, for real," she confessed, voice riddled with terror.

Careful not to downplay her feelings, I pulled her into a comforting hug. "Tell me everything. What happened after I left the party? Did someone try to hurt you?"

"I–I have to show you something."

"What?"

"Follow me."

I trailed behind Jade to the kitchen and watched her open the freezer door, reach in, and pull out a black velvet bag I knew wasn't there prior. She turned the bag upside down, and we watched ten diamonds dance across my granite countertop.

My eyes bulged wide. "What. The. Fuck."

"I know…"

"Where did you get these from?!" I exclaimed, my heart rate escalating.

She eased out a breath. "It's a long story."

I clenched my jaw, sensing the danger. "Talk fast."

"Listen, dancing is cool, aight? It's what I love to do, but there's always more money to be made."

"And that's why you work at your family's nail shop, right?"

"That ain't the type of money I'm talkin' about, Skai. I'm talkin' stacks."

Wrinkle lines crowded my forehead. "What all have you been doing to get money, Jade?"

"Chill, it's not like that, aight? You know I already get paid to sell a fantasy, but aside from that, I'm what you'd call a scout for Bankx, my boss, down at the club."

"What do you do as his scout?"

"It's simple. All I gotta do is be pretty and keep my listening ears on, and if I hear of anything important, I let Bankx know, and he breaks me off with some extra cash."

I discharged a grunted breath, knowing there was more to the story. "It's that simple, huh?"

"Yeah, simple as that. You'd be surprised how loose lips get around ass and titties."

I shifted uncomfortably, moving my weight from one leg to the other. "How long have you been doing this?"

"For about six months, I already got a nice lil' stash saved up."

"So, if all you do is listen and report back to Bankx, why haven't you told me about it before?" I quizzed, calling bullshit.

Her gaze tore down to the floor. "Because sometimes it's a little more than that."

"Jade, you need to be straight with me. Where the fuck did you get these diamonds, and what the fuck are you really into down at that club?"

Air hissed through a crack in her tight lips. "Sometimes me and a couple of the other girls do jobs for Bankx for some *real* premium pay."

"Jobs? What kind of jobs?"

"We just flirt and drink, and when the mark passes out, we may have a look around his spot."

My eyes widened. "You're *robbing* niggas, Jade? Are you fucking crazy? Do you know how dangerous that shit is?"

"Calm down, Skai! This is exactly why I never told you! I knew you'd overreact!"

"I have every right to overreact, Jade! Do you hear what the hell you're telling me right now? How the fuck did you even get roped into some shit like this?"

"Listen, Skai. I was careful, okay? Besides, those niggas are so zooted out of their minds that they barely know their mouths from their assholes. And in the morning, they don't remember shit. By the time they realize shit is missing, we're like distant memories."

Air left my nostrils in a rush. "Who did you rob, Jade? Was it someone from the party?"

She bobbed her head. "Yeah."

"Who?"

"It's not important."

"Bullshit! You robbed a nigga and then came here! What if someone followed you, huh?"

"The only reason I even came here is because you're the only person I trust, and no one knows where you live!"

"Who did you rob, Jade? Tell me right now!" I demanded.

Her chest caved with an exhale. "The one who hired me. Y'know, the one I told you about that I met at the club prior."

I closed my eyes, and Baby's face immediately popped into my head. "Shit," I whispered.

"What?"

"Is his name Baby or something like that?"

Jade looked at me with concern etched across her face. "How do you know him?"

"I don't, but we met and talked briefly outside on the balcony, so there's a possibility that he knows what I look like! Fuck!"

I tossed my head back and groaned. Suddenly, her problem had become *our* problem, and I didn't want any part of that life. *I knew I should've stayed my ass in the fuckin' house*, I thought to myself.

"Look, the likelihood of him remembering anything is slim to none, Skai. He was passed out on the floor when we left."

"But what if he does, huh? You can't stand here and tell me the thought hasn't crossed your mind. Why else would you come running to my door all paranoid and shit? He could be sitting outside my apartment right now waiting for you or me to come outside and blast our heads off for what YOU did!" I accused with my finger wagging in the air.

"Listen, the money was one thing, but I didn't *plan* to steal the diamonds, okay? I was just cleaning out the safe, and when I felt around in the back, there they were."

"And you decided it would be a good idea to fucking take them?"

"I don't know what the fuck came over me! It all happened so fast. I saw them, slid the bag inside my panties, finished emptying the safe, and dipped."

"So, no one knows you have them beside us?"

"No one," she assured me.

"And, you're sure? What about the girls you worked with?"

"It was only one other girl, and that bitch didn't see shit. But it's not her I'm worried about. It's Bankx."

"What would Bankx come after you for? He got what he was supposed to get out of it, right?"

"Yeah, but you didn't see how he looked at me. It was like he knew they were missing."

"The diamonds? Did he specifically ask for them?"

"No, but I don't know. I can feel it in my gut. It was like he was testing me, and if he finds out I held out on him, he'll kill me, Skai."

"How do you know that?"

"You don't know him like I do. He's not one to be fucked with. I heard he killed his own father when he was fourteen."

"So, then you can't run, Jade! You have to keep going on like everything is normal until we figure out a plan. I mean, I don't know. Bankx sounds like a crazy person to me. Can't we talk to the cops or something? Ask for protection?"

"And say what? That I robbed a nigga for another nigga? And kept that nigga's diamonds for myself? Use that fuckin' big brain of yours, Skai! Besides, I'm too fuckin' pretty to go to jail," she hissed.

"Then what the fuck are you gonna do, Jade?"

"I don't fucking know, okay? Shit! Just let me think!" Jade scolded before reaching out to grab my arms. "We gotta run, Skai. Throw whatever you can in a bag, and we'll just go!"

I pulled away from her. "We? Jade, I love you, you know I do, but I still have to go to work. It's my second year of residency, Jade. I can't just up and disappear. I'll lose my job, and then what? I–I can't just up and quit my life because of a decision YOU made! Besides, I already told you that you couldn't run! Because if you do, he'll know you lied, Jade! Is that what you want?"

"I can't just sit here and wait for one of them niggas to catch up to me after they find out what I did! No, fuck this. I gotta go!"

"Jade."

"Ba still has connections to family in Vietnam. I can leave the country, maybe lay low in Mexico for a few weeks, and then go there. I just gotta think!"

"Jade," I repeated.

"No, no. I–I have to hide the diamonds until I can figure out what to do with them!"

"Jade!" I agonized, trying to pull her out of her mangled and irrational thought process.

"What?" she screamed back at me before frantically placing each diamond back in the bag and shoving them back inside the freezer.

"Jade, what are you doing? Y–you can't leave them here."

"Just until I figure out what to do with them, okay? Do you have a better idea?"

"I don't know!" I screamed. "I didn't ask for any of this! YOU put this on me! You brought death to my doorstep!"

"Skai, I—"

"No! I can't believe you used me! The only reason you wanted me at that party was so that you could use me as a distraction! I thought we were friends, Jade!"

Tears began to slide down her cheeks. "We are! I swear to you. I— I'm sorry, okay? You're right. You're right. I never *ever* should've gotten you involved, and I shouldn't have come here. I'm just scared, girl. What if they both end up coming after me?"

I reluctantly shook my head. "It won't come down to that."

"Please, Skai. Please," she begged, "you're the only one I have in my corner."

My lips twisted into a frown. "Only until we figure out something else."

She pulled me into a tight hug. "Thank you, girl. I love you. Best bitches for life?"

Hugging her back, I replied, "Best bitches for life, and I love you, too."

"I'm sorry I kept all this from you for so long, but I thought it was best to keep you and anybody close to me in the dark. You know a real bitch ain't never supposed to tell *all* her business."

My head shook from left to right, unable to settle the thoughts bouncing around in my brain. "Yeah, my mind is blown. Like, I feel like I need a drink, and it's nowhere near the appropriate time of day for that," I remarked, making my way over to the curtains to take a peek outside.

Although she'd done a good job of shutting out the sunlight, I could see bits of rays popping out from underneath the curtains.

"If Bankx is as dangerous as you say he is, we need to think of a solid plan, Jade," I announced from across the room.

"I know. I–" Before she could complete her answer, my phone began to ring.

"Shit," I grumbled while looking at the screen.

She flinched. "What? What is it?"

"It's the hospital. I gotta go in."

"What? No! You can't leave me, Skai!"

Torn between a rock and a hard place, I sighed. "Listen, I'll check on you as soon as I can. We can even stay on the phone from the minute I leave to the time I get to the hospital, okay? And I'll triple lock the door behind me. You're safe here, Jade. Nothing is going to happen to you, okay?" I asked, gently gripping her shoulders.

She nodded sluggishly. "Yeah, okay."

"You take a shower and try to get some rest. I promise we'll figure this out as soon as I get back."

One twelve-hour shift and four coffees later, I finally arrived home. As tired as my body was, my mind was still buzzing with all the information Jade had laid on me before I left. I didn't know what the hell she was going to do, but I was going to make sure we figured something out together.

"Jade?" I called out as soon as I opened the door. "Where are you? I'm back!" I continued before flicking the light switch.

The minute the room illuminated, my face turned pallid, and my pulse escalated somewhere around the 180 mark. Standing in the middle of my living room floor was the beautiful creature I'd met on that balcony the night before. Only this time, Baby's warm brown eyes were as cold as the steel he had his trigger finger wrapped around. Hair lifted on the nape of my neck. I could tell by the stubborn set of his jaw that he was a dangerous man to cross.

"Close the fuckin' door, gorgeous. We need to talk."

BABY

She didn't scream.

She didn't run.

She didn't do shit but stare into my eyes.

Even with all the rage tussling inside me, I couldn't tear my eyes away from hers. Our silent standoff dragged on for thirty seconds before I inched forward. The wood floor squeaked underneath her as she instinctively took a step back, pressing her back against the wall before locking her knees in place.

I watched panic spread through her body as her chin trembled. Her anxious forehead signaled she was about to break out in hysterics at any second. "H–how did you get in here? W–where is s–she?" she asked as quiet as a shadow on the ground.

Frustrated, the muscle in my right cheek flexed. "You tell me. And while you at it, tell me where the fuck all my shit is before I have to put a bullet in your pretty ass," I warned, heat flushing through my body. She didn't understand how enraged I was. I was ready to shoot her best friend in the fuckin' face for stealing from me.

Worry lines framed her mouth and tugged at her fearful russet brown eyes. "D—did you h–hurt h–her?" she stuttered in a reluctant tone.

I inched another step closer, getting a whiff of her jasmine perfume. She flinched but kept her back glued to the wall.

"H–how'd you find us?"

I kept my chin high and legs planted wide. "Wasn't hard," I answered, keeping my voice steady. "Besides, that shit don't fuckin' matter. You the one askin' all the questions when I'm the one that came here lookin' for fuckin' answers."

She didn't need to know that I had the owner run the cameras back from the bachelor party, and I ran my cameras back from the entry of my apartment and saw myself stumbling inside with those hoes. My brothers got the I.D.s of all the girls, and I tracked Jade and Skai to that apartment.

"Y—you really don't know wh—where she is?"

"If I did, I wouldn't be standing here shooting the shit with you," I retorted.

"I–I'm sorry. I don't know where she is either."

"Why the fuck should I trust you, huh? You came into the party with that hoe. As far as I'm concerned, birds of a feather."

"No! I swear I didn't know what Jade and her friend were into or what they would do to you!"

Her choice of words seemed to bait me in hopes I'd draw my own conclusions. "But you do know that they were into something."

My eyes narrowed as I searched her face and studied her mannerisms. Her shoulders were wound as tight as a yo-yo, and she was tapping her right leg to calm her nerves. She was gripping her phone so tight that her knuckles had turned white. I quickly smacked it away from her hand and watched it sail across the floor.

Anger crept into my voice. "Don't try to be fuckin' slick," I warned, aware of the panic feature on the iPhone. "Tell me where the fuck your friend is! That bitch got somethin' that belongs to me."

Her brows jumped up before she darted toward the kitchen. I cocked my gun. "Ay! Slow the fuck down!"

She shot her hands up in the air and froze. "I–I think I have what you came for. Just, p–please d–don't sh–shoot me," she begged, "t–they're in the freezer."

"What's in the freezer?" I quizzed, finger itching to pull the trigger.

"Y–your diamonds."

My ears perked up. Pistol aimed at her back; I nodded for her to proceed. "You better not be fuckin' with me."

No sooner than she swept her hand across her forehead, new beads of sweat repopulated. "I'm not. I swear!"

I watched her stick her arm deep into the back of her freezer before her breathing started to come in ragged gasps. "Oh shit," she mumbled.

"What?"

Frozen dinners, a tub of ice cream, and packages of frozen peas and broccoli filled her countertop before she stopped her search. "They're gone."

My temple twitched. "What the fuck you mean they're *gone*? So that bitch still has my fuckin' diamonds!"

"They were here when I left! I swear they were!"

I charged toward her, closing the space between us before I snatched her work badge from her chest and slid it into my pocket. "I told you not to fuck with me, didn't I?"

"Please, listen to me! I'm not fucking with you! I'll tell you anything you want to know, I swear. Just, p–please put the gun down. I don't know where Jade is. I'm just as lost as you are!"

"Call that bitch!" I roared, gun steady in my grasp.

"Okay, okay! Just let me get my phone!" she screamed.

"And put that shit on speaker!" I demanded.

She hurried across the room to pick up her phone. I observed her trying to focus her sad eyes on a space somewhere in the air between us while we listened to the phone ring twice before going to voicemail.

"It's your girl, Jade. I can't make it to the phone because a bitch is out here livin' life! Leave a message, and maybe I'll call you back."

She abruptly ended the call. "No answer."

"Man, fuck!"

The phone shook in her clammy palms as she attempted to call again. "Come on, Jade. Pick up. Please, please pick up," she pleaded before ending the call. "I don't know what to do."

"You said you ain't know what your girl was into, but what all do you know?" I asked.

"It would be easier for me to talk to you if there weren't a gun pointed at my face."

Eyeing her again, I noticed that she was still shaking. There was no doubt in my mind that she was green.

I lowered my gun and glared at her with my teeth gritted. "Start talking."

Her lips parted, hands still raised to keep the distance between us. "All I know is that sometimes she and the other girls do jobs for their boss, and in return, he pays them."

"Hold up, their boss? Bankx?"

Her brow constricted. "Wait, how do you know Bankx?"

"We got history."

"What kind of history?"

"That's none of your concern," I replied, head shaking from left to right.

"Except for in this case, what I don't know might actually get my best friend or me killed," she stated, arms folded across her chest.

"And what you gon' do with that information, huh? You can't run to the cops. As much as you don't wanna be in this, you're in it now, gorgeous. And if I don't get them fuckin' diamonds back, there's gon' be hell to pay for everybody."

"W–what do you mean?"

The fearful look in her eyes made me want to put everything on the line to protect her. It was unfamiliar and made me feel more uncomfortable than a mothafucka.

My nostrils pushed out an exasperated sigh. "All you need to know is the diamonds she stole from me weren't mine to take, but they may as well have my name written all over them."

"Whose were they?" I eyed her, waiting for the dots to connect in her head. "Shit," she grumbled.

"Yeah, exactly, and if I tracked you and your girl down in less than twenty-four hours. What makes you think he won't do the same? And if he finds her before I do, it's gonna be a problem," I warned her.

Bankx had made it clear where he stood. He was tryna put my brothers and me on the menu to devour one by one. There was no doubt in my mind that he would connect the dots and be on Jade's ass just as much as I was. The truth was, she'd made enemies on both sides of those diamonds. It was only a matter of time before one of us caught up with her.

"Can you help me find her?"

A line slashed across my forehead. "What?"

"Listen, wherever Jade is, so are those diamonds, so help me help you," she suggested. The silence filled the void between us while I stared at her. "Please. I've never seen her like that. She was genuinely scared."

"She should be. The bitch is in over her head, and so are you."

"Please."

My stern glare softened a bit. "Let's go."

SKAI

Ten minutes later, I was sitting inside his ride, heart thudding against the seatbelt as I twisted my fingers in my lap. The distinct aroma of marijuana hung inside his ride like a cloud as Young Dolph blared from his car speakers. He cleared the side streets, and twenty minutes after that, we were in the parking lot of Ba's nail shop. Before I knew it, an hour had passed, and we'd driven past Ba's nail shop, her apartment, and the club. There was no sign of Jade's car, and her phone was still going straight to voicemail. He pulled into an abandoned parking lot a few blocks away from the club and killed the engine. I waded through the lengthy silence; my mind flooded with questions about where she could be. We'd seemingly hit a brick wall.

"I don't know where she could be."

A flicker of irritation and impatience shone in his eyes. "The clock is ticking," he warned, "and for once, I'm not the bad guy here."

"Yeah, well, neither am I. It was supposed to be a fun night out," I mumbled while gripping my hands together in my lap.

"How you get wrapped up in all this shit anyway? I mean, you don't look like the type to keep the same company as your girl."

"Just because we're different doesn't mean she's a bad person, aight?"

His eyes rolled skyward. "Yeah, okay. Tell that to my missing shit."

I snapped my neck in his direction with a grimace across my face. He was only thinking about himself and what he'd lost, while I was the only one with genuine concerns about Jade's whereabouts and well-being. A part of what he said did have truth to it. From the outside looking in, no one would have thought Jade and I were supposed to run in the same circles. I wasn't into the same things or made the same choices as she did, and yet somehow, I'd ended up tangled in her web right next to Baby. But he didn't know her like I did; no one did.

"Look, I'm not condoning what she did, but do you really not see the part you played in all of this?"

"What you mean? Those bitches played me! I'm the victim in this shit!" he protested.

"All I'm saying is, you didn't seem to be feeling any pain when we crossed paths. You were blowing money and partying until the blue of the morning. Maybe you had a hand in making yourself the target."

His face became stern. "Just because I put my gun down, don't be feelin' all comfortable enough to start talkin' shit," he replied with a grunt.

I raised my eyes and looked at him curiously. "Is it talkin' shit if it's the truth?"

I caught him turning away and smirking at my comment before he changed the subject. "Yeah, whatever. What else did your girl tell you about that nigga, Bankx?"

A vein throbbed on my forehead. "I've already told you everything she told me. He sounds dangerous."

"If that's all you know about Bankx, then you don't know shit. That mothafucka is dangerous, but he ain't as dangerous as me," he warned.

Feeling overwhelmed, I leaned forward and cradled my face in my palms. "I don't flex. I don't beef. I save fuckin' lives for a living, and yet here I am! All I want to do is find my best friend, get you what you came for, and be done with this entire thing!"

"Yeah. The sooner I get my shit back, the sooner all of this will go away."

"But what if it doesn't? You said you two got history, right?"

"What about it? That ain't got nothing to do with you."

"But what if it has something to do with Jade now because of what she did? Just how dangerous is he? What will he do if he finds out and connects us all?"

"That's why we need to catch up with your girl to stop that from happening."

"What makes him so dangerous?"

"Years ago, he was a well-known Miami hustler. I was nothing but a lil' guppy when my brother brought me around, and we first started working under him. Shit, I woke up every morning ready for the danger. Ready to soak up the game like a mah'fuckin' sponge, y'know? Everything was good until my brother started dating his younger sister, Jhene. Then, everything changed. There was just this unspoken beef between them, to the point where they couldn't be in the same room together. Because of that, Bankx started taking me under his wing, showing me more of the game and letting me make moves and shit. And then, one day, it all stopped."

Intrigued, I asked, "What happened?"

"The Feds raided a couple of his spots and recovered over fifty grams of coke, a couple of ounces of marijuana, cash, scales, guns, ammo, all that shit."

"Wow."

"Yeah. The minute they rounded him up, the word on the street became all about how my brother was the one who had a hand in taking him down."

"Did he?"

He cut his eyes at me. "Hell nah. Their beef was always more one-sided. Rome was not trying to let it spill over into business, but it happened anyway."

"So, if he didn't have anything to do with setting him up, why'd you steal his diamonds?"

He sighed, twisting his neck from side to side before answering my question. "A few days before the Feds rounded him up, I overheard his plans to have my brother set up to move him out of the way in business and away from his sister. It became fuck that nigga after that. You not gon' threaten my blood's life and try to take food off his plate and think I'm the type of nigga to let that shit slide. Nah, I was gon look out for mine and make sure we were all straight while that nigga rotted behind bars."

"How'd you even know about the diamonds or where to find them?"

"I told you, after his fall out with Rome, he started leaning on me a lot more. I was privy to a lot more shit than anyone realized. You'd be surprised how many people don't take a young, reckless nigga seriously. I only regret not realizing how far his reach was from behind bars."

"What do you mean?"

He sighed. "The night of Rome's birthday, he and his girl were leaving the club when niggas shot up his fuckin car when she was inside."

I placed my hand over my mouth. "Oh my God. What happened to her? Did she survive?"

"Nah. She ain't make it," he answered before twisting his neck to look outside the window. My eyes caught a glimpse of the name Jasmin tattooed on the side of his neck before I spoke. "I'm sorry."

"Yeah." We sat engulfed in a few seconds of silence before he caught me glancing at him just a little longer than I should've. "What you doin' sittin' over there like you got somethin' to say?"

Air escaped from my throat. "Who's Jasmin? If you don't mind me asking."

"Nobody."

"So, you just get anyone's name scraped into your skin?"

"She's nobody anymore," he rephrased.

"Mmm. Old love, huh?"

"If that's what you wanna call it."

"What else am I supposed to call it? And if it's over, why'd you keep it?"

"I used to keep it because I thought she'd come to her senses and make her way back to me, but now I keep this shit as a reminder to never give my heart away again."

My eyebrows stretched for my hairline. His unexpected confession was deep enough to drown in yet refreshing enough to revive me. "Wow, that was surprisingly deep."

"What about you? What's your love story?"

My left shoulder rose and fell. "Love story? I don't have one."

"Why not?"

"I don't know. Guess I was tired of meeting the same nigga in different bodies, so I quit altogether."

"Mmm."

"What's that mean?" I quizzed.

"I bet you ain't never met a nigga like me before."

"You're probably right about that, but drug dealers ain't my thing, so...."

He scoffed. "That's supposed to offend me?"

"That depends. Are you offended?" My eyes tangled with his for a few seconds before his gaze dropped to my lips. I realized he'd been watching me talk, and I instantly became nervous.

"Not at all. Opinions are like assholes; everybody got one."

"That may be true, but I mean, it's not a lifestyle built for longevity."

"Trust me; I know that."

"So, what's the end game?"

"Not gettin' killed and not gettin' caught," he answered with a relaxed shrug of his shoulders.

Before I had a chance to rebuttal, my phone began to vibrate in my lap. We both looked down to see Jade's photo on the screen. "Oh shit!" I yelped, hurriedly sliding to accept. "H—hello? Jade? Oh my God, Jade! Where are you? Please tell me where you are!"

I put the phone on speaker, awaiting her responses to my

questions. I had a feeling it was the difference between life and death. "H—hello? Jade? Are you there?"

I could hear what sounded like gurgling or choking on the other line, but what I couldn't hear was her voice. The skin on the back of my neck puckered. I felt in my gut that something was wrong.

"Jade! Please tell me where you are, and I'll come to you right now!" I pleaded.

Before I could get an answer, the line went dead. My hands began to shake all over again, and it was the first time I realized they'd stopped somewhere in mid-conversation with him.

"I think something's wrong," I told him.

"Try tracking her phone now," he suggested before starting the engine.

Jade's phone pinged near two rundown motels about eleven minutes from where we were. Gun in hand, Baby threw the car in park and hopped out before I could unhook my seatbelt. Desperate to find Jade and put my worries to rest, I darted inside both motels, asking the attendants if they'd seen her. Neither of them had. When I popped out of the second motel entrance, I saw Baby coming out of the shadows from the alleyway that separated the debilitated establishments. I met him halfway.

"Get in the car."

"What? Did you find her?"

"No. Get in the car," he demanded, eyes stationed on me.

"What the hell is down there? What did you see? Is she back there?" I asked, shuffling forward. "Jade? Jade! Where are you?"

He drilled his feet into the ground in front of me before clamping his hand around my frail wrist and dragging me closer to him until his chest was mashed against mine. "You don't want to go down there," he forewarned me, brows sloped high.

"What do you mean? What's down there? Where's Jade?" I rambled, trying to break past him.

Concern pinwheeled across his face. "Just get back in the car."

Our eyes engaged, and the same shaky feeling reappeared in the center of my gut. One eyebrow crept toward my hairline. Something wasn't right. "What? No. Tell me what's going on! Was Jade back there? Jade? Jade!" I called out over his shoulder.

His voice hardened as he spoke. "Get back in the fuckin' car, Skai."

"No!" I shouted before darting past him.

I hadn't come all that way to leave without Jade. My feet hurried down the alleyway only to come to a chilling halt. I slapped a hand over my mouth as my eyes soaked in the horror in front of me. My eyes slowly started to become bloodshot while tears populated at the rim of my eyes. "J–Jade?"

My lip trembled as I drew in a sharp breath and held it, trying to stop myself from completely falling apart. There she was, throat slit and bleeding out onto the pavement. Hands trembling, I dropped to my knees to reach out and touch her hand. Her body was lukewarm. "Don't worry, Jade. Don't you worry. I'm gonna get you to the hospital, and I'm going to fix this. I'm going to fix you, okay? You're gonna be okay. Don't worry," I assured her as tears leaked out of my eyes.

I hurriedly dialed 9-1-1 while trying to secure her airway and stop the bleeding. It was dark, but I could see her exposed vocal cords. My heart was beating so fast I started to feel faint and breathless as all the color receded from my cheeks. More tears rose up in my throat, but I managed to quell them.

"Shit! C'mon, Jade. Don't leave me. Please don't leave me."

"9-1-1, what's your emergency?" the operator asked.

"Y–yes. I need an ambulance at the alleyway near 9183 Caliver Cove. I have a twenty-seven-year-old female with a homicidal cut to her anterior neck. She's lost a significant amount of blood, and her vocal cords are exposed. I've been trying to stop the bleeding, but I–I can't secure her airway. Please send help immediately! Her name is Jade Tran."

"Okay, ma'am. I'm sending paramedics to your location now. Please just stay on the–"

Before she could finish her sentence, Baby appeared behind me and ended the call. "We have to go," he announced.

I cut my sorrowful eyes at him. "I'm not leaving her."

"You did all you could do. Staying here ain't gon' do shit but bring more problems to your doorstep. We gotta go!"

"No! She's not gone yet. I can still save her! I just need to stay with her until the paramedics arrive!"

"We can't fuckin' be here when they arrive, Skai."

"I'm NOT leaving her!" I protested.

Jaw and shoulders tense, he gallantly charged forward and wrapped his strong arms around my torso. In the blink of an eye, he'd pinned my body beneath his muscled arms, tossed me over his shoulder and carried me back to the car before speeding off.

"We have to go back! I can't leave her! I don't care what happens to me! Please just take me back!" I screamed, hearing the echo of sirens howling in the distance.

"But what if I do?"

As I stared out of the window, my eyes slowly started to glisten again. "Sh–she's not going to make it, is she?" I whispered, a dreadful fear gripping my throat as the words emerged.

He sloped his head to the left, non-verbally answering my question. Soon, I began to sniffle as fresh tears fell into my lap. My clothes were soaked with her blood and secretions.

"W–where are you taking me?" I asked. I'd been too busy drowning in my sorrows to notice where we were going.

"My place," he grumbled quietly.

Grief sat heavily on my face as I slightly bowed my head. "You don't have to do that. I–I'll be okay."

The landscape of his face said he pitied me. "You can't go nowhere lookin' like that. You can sleep at my spot for the night, take a shower, and get your head together. In the morning, I'll take you wherever you wanna go."

His apartment was in the clouds in a high-rise in South Beach. After exiting the elevator, I stood rooted to the hardwood floor by the doorway while he disappeared down the hallway for a couple of minutes. I ignored what button he'd pressed in the elevator, but with his 360-degree view of the city, I knew Jesus had to be his next-door neighbor.

"Here," he offered, tossing me a T-shirt and a pair of basketball shorts. "You can put these on after your shower. Bathroom is the first door on the left."

I reached out to take the clothes. My hands still hadn't stopped shaking. "T–thank you."

Ten minutes later, I was standing under the hot water, shaking and moaning in pain. My chest heaved in and out as my eyes pumped a steady stream of tears. There was less than a ten percent chance that Jade survived, and it killed me that I couldn't be anywhere near her to fix her or at least hold her hand. She didn't deserve to die alone. Jade was the very best and worst parts of me. She'd always been a true friend to me. Y'know, the type of person I could trust with my deepest secrets and didn't have to watch what I said around her. She wasn't the type to hold it against me if I had too much to drink and decided to show my ass. She'd simply pull my hair back or tell me to wrap it up if I was going to have some late-night company. My lashes were heavy with tears, making it hard to see as I scrubbed her blood off my hands. I still hadn't figured out how in the hell I landed in the predicament I was in. I stepped out of the shower, skull pounding from all the crying. After drying off, I sat on the edge of the toilet and called around to every nearby hospital to check to see if Jade had been admitted, but none had been able to identify her. Which meant there was a strong chance that Jade was dead.

Tears started again without sound or movement when my bare feet tipped out of the bathroom and back to the living room. I quickly wiped them away when I saw that Baby's eyes had landed on mine. With my posture hunched and my eyes and nose running like a leaky faucet, I was a mess.

"She's gone," I sobbed.

A look of discomfort passed over his features before he lowered his gaze to the floor. Hours prior, he wanted to be the one to put a bullet in her for what she'd done to him. I couldn't blame him for not feeling anything about her being gone.

"I'm sorry," he answered finally.

"H–hey, um. D–do you have any Tylenol? My head is killing me."

He dipped his chin before opening one of his matte black kitchen cabinets and pulling out a bottle of Tylenol, then filled a glass with fresh, ice-cold water. "Here."

Ice clinked gently in the glass as I rolled it absently between my hands. I tossed the pills down my throat and took a couple of sips before the glass slipped from my grasp and shattered against the marble floor. I gasped while stepping back. "Shit! I'm sorry! I'll clean it up."

He looked into my eyes before flipping my hands over to check for any cuts. "Are you okay?"

"I'm fine. I'm sorry I'm such a fucking mess," I confessed.

Baby gently tilted my chin and looked into my eyes before reassuring me it was okay. "Go in the living room. I'll clean this up."

"Are you sure?"

"I'm sure."

A few minutes later, he brought out a fresh glass of ice water and set it on the coffee table, then returned with a heated blanket he'd pulled from the dryer and laid it over me.

"Maybe this will stop you from shaking," he observed, hand resting on my shoulder a beat too long. "Try and get some sleep."

I glanced up at him. "Thanks."

"Goodnight," he replied before flipping off the lights.

"Baby?"

"Yeah?"

"I'm sorry you had to catch me on the worst night of my life," I quavered into the darkness.

"Tomorrow's a new day," he answered.

BABY

I WOKE UP THE FOLLOWING DAY WITH THE SAME UNSORTED FEELINGS nagging at me. From the moment Skai flipped on that light and saw me standing in her apartment, something inside me felt the urge to protect her. I listened to her toss, turn, and sob in the darkness for hours until some unconscious process forced her to shut down, let her mind go blank, and fall asleep. She'd lost someone close to her, and I wouldn't dare tell her shit was gon' be alright because it wouldn't have been anytime soon. I put my thoughts about Skai aside to focus on a bigger issue. The diamonds were gone, and the bitch who'd stolen them from me was dead, which meant there was a high chance that Bankx had them back in his possession.

I tapped Rome's name and pressed the phone to my ear when the line started to ring. He answered with sleep heavy in his voice. "Hello?" he grumbled.

"Yo. You still sleep?" I asked, pulling the phone away to look at the time.

"A nigga been on daddy duty all night. RJ got a cold."

"Damn, yo. Hope lil' man feel better."

"Yeah, he'll be aight. What's up?"

"Look, I found one of the girls who robbed me. The one who took the diamonds."

"And?"

"She's dead, and before you ask, that body ain't on me."

"If not you, then who?" The line fell silent for a few seconds while I waited for him to answer his question himself. "Shit."

"Yeah. The diamonds weren't on her, which means–"

"He's gotta know," he answered.

I rubbed the back of my head. I knew Bankx was nothin' to fuck with, but neither were we. "Yeah."

"Man, fuck!" he yelled. "Aight, just keep me posted. I'ma get up with Chief and call you later."

"Aight."

After I got off the phone with my brother, I headed into the kitchen to start making myself something to eat. Skai was lying still across the couch, so I figured I'd let the smell of fresh coffee and a meal wake her. After a few bites into my sandwich, Skai glided into the kitchen as if she didn't weigh more than a feather.

"Besides the coffee, what smells so good in here?" she inquired.

"Medianoche," I answered as I took another bite.

She frowned. "What does that mean?"

"It means midnight sandwich. You want some?"

"I'm not hungry," she replied, twisting her neck from side to side.

"You need to eat. Here, take a bite."

I extended the other half of my sandwich to her and held my hand under her chin so that nothing hit the floor.

She forced a smile. "It's delicious. What's on it?" she asked around a mouthful of sandwich.

"It's kinda like a Cuban sandwich; ham, Swiss, roast beef, and shit, but the bread is softer and sweeter."

"Where'd you learn how to make this?"

"Back when we were growing up, Mama would make us these all

the time before she left for work. With a house full of boys always eating up everything in sight, medianoches were the quickest and easiest thing to make."

"Well, for what it's worth, I think I found my new favorite sandwich."

I tossed out a joke. "Upgrading from PB&J's, huh?"

She sucked her teeth before a wry little smile quirked her mouth. "How'd you know?"

"But for real, how'd you sleep? I heard you tossing and turning a lot," I stated, giving her a once-over. With dark circles and puffy eyes, she looked like a boxer who'd been tagged and didn't want to show it. Even a blind man could see that the pain had hit her like a Mack truck.

She shook her head before answering, "Not good. I kept thinking about how I needed to call Ba about Jade, but I don't know if I can face him right now. Like, how do I tell her family she's dead and that I left her in an alleyway with her throat slit like a coward?"

"You're far from a coward, Skai."

She scoffed. "Tell that to my conscious."

Guilt was gnawing at her soul like a rodent's teeth. I knew from experience it would take a while for her heartache to go numb.

"I hope you don't blame yourself for what happened to your friend. She knew the shit she was doing could catch up to her one day. You can't carry that load on your shoulders. There's no way you could've known what was gon' happen."

She shook her head as a single tear slipped down her face. Her hand quickly swatted it away before she groaned. "Ugh! I'm so fucking tired of crying! But I just wish I could've done more, y'know? She deserved better. She deserved so much more from me."

"Can I tell you somethin'?"

"What is it?"

"Aight, so real talk, I don't remember a lot from the night we met, but what I do remember is you tellin' me you were a doctor. I thought that shit was all cap until I stood back and watched you spring into action and try to save someone's life, yo. Plus, you called 9-1-1, Skai. What more do you think you could've done? You're not God."

She lifted a sulky shoulder. "I guess we'll never know now."

We both finished our sandwiches in silence before I spoke up again. "So, you figure out where you wanna go?"

"What?"

"I told you last night I'd take you wherever you wanted to go."

Her shoulder bobbed. "It's like I don't know anything anymore. Home was where I felt the safest, and now I'm scared to go back there. What if Bankx is looking for me, too?"

"To be honest, I don't think you gotta worry about that nigga. He got what he was after. I think it's over, for you at least."

Concern floated over her face. "And what about you?"

"Don't worry about me. I can handle myself."

"You didn't find the diamonds on her, did you?" she asked, a frown tangling her brow.

My face contracted into tight lines. "Nah. But I told you, I'll be fine."

"I wish I had your confidence."

"Don't worry, Baby got you," I assured her while patting my chest. "By my side, you're always safe."

"At the party, you told me your real name was Judah, right?"

"Damn, I must've been faded just to be giving out my government like that."

Her features went lax with a soft smile. "Yeah."

"What about it?"

A shrug rolled over her shoulders. "I don't feel right calling a grown-ass man, Baby. I think Judah suits you better. Or maybe just Ju for short."

"Ju, huh?"

"Yeah," she agreed with a bob of her chin.

Skai stood frozen, staring brazenly into my eyes while resting her right elbow against my countertop. "What?" I quizzed.

"Just, thank you," she expressed with the upturn of a smile, "for everything."

65

A smile took possession of my lips, although I was still unsure how I felt about her. A part of me knew the best thing for the both of us would be to stay far away from each other in case of any blowback from Bankx, but I didn't know if I was willing to leave her alone just yet.

SKAI

TWO DAYS LATER.

A full forty-eight hours passed before I returned to work. I spent my first day back trying to pretend everything was as normal as possible, throwing myself into my work more and more, trying to put my energy and my brain on something other than how fucking sad I was. Every fiber of my body was taut with grief. I kept my head low for the first half of the day, only coming alive to prep for rounds, check in on my patients, and update their charts.

"Did you hear?" Kelsea approached me to my left.

"What?"

"I'm scrubbing in on a craniotomy in forty-five fucking minutes!" She beamed.

My eyebrows rose in a slow arch as I tried to force a half-smile, knowing my eyes were empty. "Wow, that's exciting."

Dr. Kelsea Shanks was the only other Black woman and fellow intern in my program year with whom I had a connection. She was a fellow general surgeon and just as intelligent and wide-eyed as me when it came to practicing medicine. As interns, we involuntarily spent much of our time together and got close-*ish* over time. We hung out outside of work occasionally, but she wasn't someone I raced to spill all my personal business to outside of my hospital drama with Malik. Those privileges had only been reserved for Jade. Kelsea knew of Jade, but I didn't make a habit of mixing the two crowds. While I was out, I had her tell the chief resident that I had the flu so I wouldn't risk getting written up. As badly as I wanted to spill my guts to someone, anyone, about what happened, what I'd been through was so traumatic I couldn't tell a soul. The only person I could talk to about it was Jade, and I'd only be able to see her in my dreams for the rest of my life.

"Plans tonight?" Kelsea asked.

"You mean besides the hot date I've got with my Netflix account?" I asked with a shrug.

She smacked her lips behind her face mask. "That sounds lonely as shit."

"Yeah, well—that's the shit I'm on," I muttered my confirmation.

"Not me. I require more than Netflix and Chill at this big age, so a nigga can feel free to come harder than that."

"If the love language ain't giving naps and snacks, then it ain't for me right now."

"Now that I feel you on. I definitely want a nap date. I'm so tired! I legit haven't had a day off since last Tuesday!"

We continued to make our way down the hall when Kelsea noticed a man wandering through the hospital corridors as if he was looking for something or someone. I craned my neck to see a bear-like, tall man with tattoos inked all over his honey-brown skin and his eyes hidden behind a pair of dark designer shades.

"What's his problem?" she wondered.

"I don't know. He looks lost."

"Excuse me, sir, can we help you?" Kelsea called out.

He sauntered closer so that I could take all of him in. Dressed in all black, he had a full, obsidian black beard that stretched from ear to ear and a perfectly lined mustache that draped around his large, pouty lips. Two large diamonds sat perched in his ears, and a gold Cuban link chain adorned his neck. His hulking body was like something out of a comic book; I took him as no less than 265 pounds.

I watched his eyes travel down to my new badge before drawing back to mine. "Actually, you're just who I've been looking for."

I shot my eyes over to Kelsea just as her brow sloped. "Are you a patient, or—"

"Where are my manners? My name is Jarrell Carter, but people call me Bankx," he introduced himself.

A cold tremor ran through my body, freezing me in place as he reached out to shake my hand. I slowly twisted my neck to Kelsea.

"Hey, Kels, I'll catch up with you in a minute, okay?"

"You sure?"

I dipped my chin, speaking bravely although I was sure the color had left my face. "Yup. I'm sure. It's cool."

"Oh, um. Okay. I'll catch up with you in a bit."

I watched her walk away with a confused look before turning my eyes back to him. I felt my palms growing clammy as my hands trembled. "I—I'm sorry, but I—I don't think that—" I stammered, failing to control my breathing.

"I'm, well, I was Jade's boss. Y'know, down at The Sanctuary," he informed me, voice low and gravely.

My eyes landed on the security camera positioned over his left shoulder. "Oh—okay. Um, what are you doing here?" I asked, trying to play it cool although my heart was pounding beneath my rib cage.

"I've been coming here for the last couple of days trying to find you. She ain't really talk about her family much, but after I heard what happened to her, I asked around at the club, and a couple of the girls told me about you and that you worked here."

"She talked to them about me?" I quizzed.

He nudged a rueful shrug. "Apparently so."

"So, um- I'm sorry, but I have to get back to work," I stated, trying to hurry past him.

He extended his hand to stop me. "Hold up. I got something for you."

I watched him reach around to his back and froze. As badly as I wanted to flee, my feet remained cemented, and my eyes trained on his large hands. All I could do was pray he didn't shoot me in cold blood in the middle of the fucking hospital.

"Please. You don't have to d—do this," I pleaded, slowly raising my hands to the height of my chest.

He pulled out a white envelope and flipped over my hand to place it in my palm before sealing my other hand on top of it. "I wanted to drop you off a lil' somethin' to show my condolences. Your girl was a real crowd-pleaser down at the club. She'll surely be missed."

My heart plummeted to the ground. "W—what is this?"

"It's to help with the funeral costs."

My lungs deflated, and suddenly I realized I'd been holding my breath. "Thanks, but I can't accept this," I denied, passing the envelope back to him.

He rested his hand on mine a little longer than I liked. The calloused skin on his palms felt rough against my own supple skin. "Your hands are like ice," he commented.

I glanced down at his strong, meaty forearm, noticing the Bible verse etched into his forearm with tattoo ink. It said, *Praise be to the Lord my rock, who trains my hands for war, my fingers for battle.* I nervously paused and turned my head before asking, "H—have you ever met a doctor with warm hands?"

He glared at me with a grin. "It's Jade's money. Take it. She earned it."

I looked down at the thick envelope before my eyes traveled back to his. Heart racing, I noted, "You never told me how you found out she was dead."

He licked his thick lips. "Bad news travels fast. Miami can be a dangerous city, especially for a beauty such as yourself. Be safe out here," he warned before turning to walk away.

I dipped my eyes down to the floor. The way the words fell off his lips had my heart ready to explode out of my chest. Was that a threat?

A promise? A general observation about the crime around the city? I had no way of knowing what he knew, but the fact that he knew of me was alarming enough. I thought my worst nightmare was over, but him showing up at my job showed me the nightmare had only just begun.

WHEN ANOTHER ONE OF MY SCOUTS INFORMED ME THAT SHE'D SPOTTED Jade, called out to her, and she ran; I knew something was up. My intuition had been correct. All the money had gone straight to her head, causing her to become reckless and make stupid decisions like trying to escape with my diamonds. I caught up with her before she could leave the city, slit her throat, and disappeared. The only payback for disloyalty in my book was death. Unfortunately, Jade was dead, and I still didn't have my diamonds. I had her locker at the club, and her apartment searched, and still nothing. After hearing some of the girls mention she had a friend who worked at the hospital, I decided to pop up on her and get a feel for what she knew. She seemed more afraid of me than anything, which was good.

Walking out of the hospital, I checked my phone to see that I'd received a text from the shorty I'd been seeing off and on for a few weeks. Bevin and I met inside my club about a month ago. She was there celebrating the end of the semester with a few of her girls. All she talked about that night was how stressed out her professors had her. She was in school getting her degree in fashion design and had a body that would've looked good in anything she put on it.

BEVIN:

Where you at?

ME:

Pullin' up now.

I pulled into her apartment complex and tapped the hazard lights on my gun metallic black Nissan Titan. Her building was located a few miles from the airport, so I leaned forward to watch the planes flying overhead, some taking off while others flew just above the trees, preparing to land. A few minutes later, Bevin approached my truck. I hopped out and made my way around to pull her into a tight bear hug. Bitches loved a big nigga, especially a big nigga with money.

"What's up, beautiful? Mmm, you smell so good," I growled before pressing my lips against her warm neck.

She giggled while melting into my arms. "Stop it."

I pulled away and let my eyes drink her in. She had long, obsidian black hair that flowed halfway down her back, a slim frame, and an ass that made a nigga consider settling down. I was in the process of rebuilding my empire brick by brick, and it would've been nice to have a beauty queen like her by my side. While running the club, I was around too much pussy daily, but I was grown enough to know that nothin' hit better than a pussy you could call home.

I glanced down at the burgundy crop top and pencil skirt set that hugged her curves in all the right places, admiring how it complemented her wheat-brown complexion. The four-inch burgundy heels she wore exposed her goddess-like feet and freshly painted cocaine-white toes.

"Damn. I think you might be out here lookin' a lil' too good today."

She smacked her pouty lips while flashing her mink brown eyes in my direction. "You got a problem with me lookin' good for you?"

"Never that."

"It's your fault for not tellin' me where we were going today. I could've toned it down a bit," she reminded me with giggles intertwining with her southern accent.

"I'll take that. C'mon, let's get out of here."

I watched her put her heel on the chrome running board to lift herself into the passenger seat before I made my way to my side.

She arched her attractive, angular brow. "Your truck is so nice. I bet you this cost like a full year of my tuition," she complimented while running her hand across the caramel-brown leather seats.

"It ain't nothin', Queen."

The engine grumbled, and I pulled off. "So, what exactly do you have planned for us today?" she inquired, eyeing the spacious interior.

My shoulders bobbed. "Whatever you wanna do for real. I was thinking maybe some shopping, take you out for dinner on a yacht." I glanced over and caught her cheesing. "That sound good to you?"

Her feathery eyelashes fluttered. "Yeah. It all sounds great."

I dipped my chin in a nod. "Bet. What does that tell you about me, then?"

"That you're the type who knows how to treat a woman right."

"Exactly. I want you to remember that."

"Why?" she quizzed, with an eyebrow arched in my direction.

"I already told you what I'm lookin' for."

"A wife, right?" she asked, pushing her long silky hair over her shoulder.

"Hell yeah."

She aimed her pointer finger at her chest. "And you think that could be me?"

"You tell me. Is that what you're looking for?"

Her gaze dropped to her lap before she drew her eyes back up to mine with her teeth displayed in a wide grin. "Ask me again at the end of our date."

JASMIN

AFTER A FULL DAY OF SHOPPING, WINING, AND DINING, BANKX DROPPED me at my apartment.

"You sure you don't wanna come up?" I asked.

He shook his head. "Nah, I got business to handle. Maybe some other time."

I bobbed my head. "Okay."

He'd been sweet enough not to pressure me into letting him come up. He was the epitome of grown and sexy; I'd give him that. He pulled up to the entrance and let the doorman grab my bags out of the backseat.

"Thanks again for today. I had a great time," I assured him, arms laced with Chanel, Louis Vuitton, and Gucci shopping bags from the Design District.

"You're welcome. I'll see you tomorrow?"

"Yes. Brunch, right?"

"Yeah."

"Okay. I'll call you when I wake up."

"Have a good night, beautiful."

I leaned in to plant a goodnight kiss on his cheek, fingertips grazing his beard. "Goodnight."

I watched him pull off before heading to my car. I typed in the coordinates to the hotel I was meeting someone at and hit the road. Bankx thought I was some naïve fashion design major named Bevin Watts when I was far from it. I was born and bred in Miami, but I left Florida for Texas when I was seventeen and never looked back. I attended college, graduating Summa Cum Laude with a bachelor's degree in criminal justice. After graduation, I got recruited by the DEA and went to Quantico, Virginia for training. From there, I started working at the DEA headquarters in Springfield, Virginia. I stayed there until I transferred to Miami's field division and joined the Organized Crime and Illegal Narcotics Enforcement Task Force three months ago. A part of me didn't know how I felt to be back in Florida after being away for so many years. Everything looked the same but different.

Forty minutes later, I made my way downtown to the hotel bar and slid my denim-clad hips across the leather seat in a secluded booth in the back. The person across from me slid his shades off, revealing his chocolate-brown eyes. He glanced down at the black and gold bracelet on my wrist. "Is that Chanel?"

I rolled my wrist back and forth, admiring my gift. "Yeah. You like?"

"It's cool, I guess."

"Even if I can't keep it forever, I'm going to enjoy it while I have it."

"How was he today?"

"Good. Sparing no expense, as you can see. Real big trick energy. I invited him up, but he didn't fall for it," I noted, knowing the apartment I was in was bugged. "He seems to be serious about settling down."

"And he wants to do it with you?"

I sat across from Miguel, silently eyeing the tattoos against his tortilla-brown skin. He tapped his fingertips against the manila folder on the table. Agent Miguel Martinez was the FBI's special agent-in-charge on the task force led by the DEA and FBI. Our mission was to disassemble illegal drug trafficking and undercover money laundering operations throughout the country, and Reynard "Big Rey" Shaw was our latest target.

He was a notorious kingpin the FBI and DEA had been chasing for years. His illegal operations were responsible for supplying and shipping numerous multi-ton loads of cocaine, marijuana, and pills throughout Atlanta, New York City, Houston, and other cities along the Texas border and Miami. We knew he used his fleet of tractor-trailers to transport packages nationwide. Agents recently intercepted several hundred kilograms of cocaine being transported across the country under the guise of his trucking company.

When word got out that his nephew, Jarrell, was released, I was added to the task force and briefed on both Reynard "Big Rey" Shaw and Jarrell "Bankx" Carter. From that moment on, every interaction with him had been calculated. My goal was to get close to him, find out what I could about his business, and the next time his uncle would send him more product. The minute we had enough information to indict, we'd take them down and start handing out indictments like candy on Halloween.

"It looks that way," I answered. "I've been talking to him for a little over a month, and his energy hasn't switched up yet, even with me playing hard to get. I've been pumping this celibacy narrative into his head so that he doesn't get any ideas. I wanna get close, but not that close, y'know?"

"He's a man. He will try you. Plus, you know better than to trust anything that comes out of his mouth. He's a self-serving scumbag."

I sucked my teeth. "This isn't my first rodeo, okay?"

He threw up his tattooed hands in surrender, his broad athletic shoulder bulging beneath his tight-fitting shirt. "You're right, my bad."

"How's your CI?" I asked, getting back to business.

"Still secure."

"And you're sure they're trustworthy?"

"Positive. You'd cooperate too when you're facing a three-year prison sentence for aggravated identity theft and unlawful possession of a credit card skimmer."

"Mmm. Okay."

He finally pushed the manila folder he'd been tapping on across the table to me with photos from a crime scene inside.

"What's this?" I asked.

"Your man's latest work."

"You're sure he did this?"

"Sure of it."

I flipped through each photo while shaking my head, including his past mugshots. I would've thought he was handsome if he hadn't been such a vicious person.

My stomach churned with sorrow. "Why'd he do this?"

"I wish I knew. He's usually careful, selective with how he handles his business but this was sloppy."

"I think he's back operating a high-traffic cocaine distribution network through that strip club full-time."

"Oh, I'm sure of it. Any idea on who his supplier is?" he asked, tone ripe with sarcasm.

"Good ol' Uncle Reynard," I confirmed.

"Exactly. Are you sure you're up for this? Because if you're not, I need to know right now. Bankx may be sweet to you, but never forget that he's a wolf in sheep's clothing, aight? He's dangerous, and he's no amateur."

"I'm here, aren't I?"

"Yeah, well—"

"Are you sure *you're* up for this?"

"We're chasing the biggest fish of them all; been chasing his ass for years, slippery mothafucka. He's got a lot of connections, too many.

We don't know who's on his payroll, and we don't have much time left. Resources equal results, Baker; without them, this operation will shrivel up a die like all the rest. That's why I need you to turn up the heat however you feel comfortable."

My skin crawled at the thought of his touch. "You want me to *fuck* him?"

Miguel looked at me like a man on a mission. "No! I didn't say that at all! Damnit, Baker! I meant get him to commit to you. He's gotta trust you before he lets you in. Tell him you're falling for him and want to try being in a relationship. Whatever you gotta do to make sure you can continue to investigate him. You think you can do that?"

I bobbed my head, knowing I couldn't take him down with simple wiretaps and bugs like they did in the old days. That was a death sentence waiting to happen. "Yeah."

"I'm tellin' you, the minute we get the information we need to take them down, I wanna nail them to the fucking wall. I'm throwing everything at them; operating a criminal enterprise, money laundering, drug conspiracy, murder, everything! I already lost my last few big cases, and I'm done takin' L's. Neither one of us can afford to fuck this up, aight?"

"I told you, I got it," I assured him while closing the folder.

He didn't have to reiterate to me how important it was. My mind was already racing with a million thoughts on my own. It wasn't my first undercover assignment but my first high-profile one. Bringing down Big Rey and his nephew meant a notch in my credibility and hopefully, more respect at the agency. I was one of the younger agents, and although I was thorough, some days I felt as if I was still trying to find my place in it all, but I was in too deep to back out. I had a lot of homework to do before the weekend ended, and I couldn't afford to fuck it up.

"That's him. I gotta go."

"Be careful," he warned.

"I will."

SKAI

I DARTED INSIDE THE LOCKER ROOM AND SHOVED THE ENVELOPE INSIDE my bag. "It doesn't exist until you get off. It doesn't exist until you get off," I repeated underneath my breath before locking it away and racing to the sink to toss some cold water on my face to calm my nerves. As soon as I hit the floor, Kelsea was waiting for me by the nurses' station. I was with her when I saw Bankx, so I knew she'd have questions.

"What was that about?" she quizzed, arching a questioning eyebrow in my direction.

"It's nothing."

She side-eyed me. "Mmhm."

"What?" I pushed.

She leaned into me. "Bitch, does your daddy know you're pussy poppin' for drug dealers?"

My eyes widened. "Excuse me? No! It's not...It's not that."

"Mmhm. Okay."

"I'm serious! I don't even know him."

"Then why was he here looking for you by name, girl?"

"Whatever."

"I'm just saying, own your shit, Skai. I know a drug dealer when I see one. I've got a sixth sense about these types of things."

"Well, you and your sixth sense can go on about your day because for the millionth time, it's not like that."

"Suit yourself. Because as for me, I love me a gangsta ass nigga that only got a soft spot for my ass. Yeaaahh, niggas like that make the pussy go woo-woo!" she joked.

We shared a laugh while making our way down the hall. "Hey, um, can you cover for me for a few hours on Thursday?"

Her eyebrow shot up before she took a sip from her coffee cup. "For what?"

"I have somewhere I need to be."

"Where? To see that *drug dealer?*" she whispered.

I smacked my teeth. "Just somewhere. Can you cover, or should I ask Parker?"

"Look, Skai, I've kept my mouth shut, but you've been different lately."

I shrugged off her accusation. "What do you mean? I'm fine."

"You're lying, Skai. We may not be besties, but we spend enough time together for me to know when you're off. I'm not saying you have to cry on my shoulder or anything, but I'm here if you wanna talk about more than lab results and charts."

I looked over both shoulders before leaning into her. "Can you keep a secret?" I asked.

She bobbed her head, and I pulled her into the nearest supply closet and shut the door.

"Skai, what the hell?"

"You remember when I told you to tell everyone I had the flu?"

"Yeah."

"Well, I didn't."

"Then what was going on?"

I sighed, not ready to say the words. "M—my um, my best friend. Sh-she um, she died," I muttered while wiping a tear from my eye. "And um, I guess it's like ever since that happened, I've just felt like I'm moving in slow motion, y'know? I mean, we're surgeons, Kelsea! I understand death. I know what it feels like to lose a parent, but this... it's just a hill I can't seem to get over, no matter how hard I try. All I wanna do is press rewind on my life and go back to a time when shit made sense! Nothing fucking makes sense anymore!" I cried.

She pulled me into a hug and started to rub my back gently. "Oh my God, Skai! I'm so sorry! Why didn't you tell me sooner?"

"It's still hard to talk about, so I've just been trying to bottle it all up, especially while I'm here."

"I get it. I do. I'm here for you if you need me."

"Thanks. That's why I need you to cover for me on Thursday. I need to attend her memorial service."

"Of course, I'll cover for you. Anything you need," she assured me.

I made sure to dry my tears before Kelsea and I exited the supply closet and made our way to the elevators at the end of the corridor. "You good?" she asked, pressing the down button.

I dipped my chin. "Yeah. One day at a time, right?"

"Exactly."

I reached out to press the up button, realizing I needed to check on my patient's labs before going to prep her for surgery. "Hey, I've got to go check on Mrs. Bowles' lab work. I'll see you later."

"Cool," she replied as the elevator dinged and the upward-facing arrow lit up first.

I stepped inside and waited for the metal doors to close before pressing the button to the fourth floor. No sooner than it started, it stopped on the next floor and opened for Malik and his fiancée, Nichelle. It was my first time seeing her in person. Before then, I'd only ever snooped on her Instagram profile. She stepped in wearing a dark blue scrub set and black Crocs on her feet. She was around my height, had chocolate brown skin and eyes, and had a similar body type to me as well—a petite build with a round ass. She wore her head full of box braids twirled up into a neat bun on the top of her head.

He froze in his step when he saw me, glitching momentarily before stepping forward as if I was nothing more than a stranger. The moment he started to open his mouth, something in my mood changed.

"Good afternoon, doctor," he greeted me with a stale voice before leaning against the elevator wall opposite of me while Nichelle stood between us.

Barely believing what was in front of me, I gave them a quick nod and a forced smile, doing my best not to make eye contact with either of them. *What the hell was she doing in Miami when she was supposed to be a fellow at Johns Hopkins in Baltimore? Did she transfer? Did he propose?* Out of pure curiosity, I shifted my eyes down to her ring finger to see if there was anything wrapped around it. *Shit,* I grumbled to myself. I was standing to her right and couldn't get a good look at her finger without being too obvious, and I wasn't about to crane my neck and seem pressed. The elevator chimed, and I stepped off with a pep in my step, trying to put as much distance between the three of us as possible without dashing off into a full sprint. Thirty minutes passed, and I was making my rounds when I heard the sound of advancing feet approaching from behind just before an unfamiliar female voice called out.

"Hi."

I turned to see Nichelle extending a cup of coffee to me. "H–hi."

"I'm Dr. Nichelle Jackson."

"Hi. I'm Dr. Daniels, um, Skai–Dr. Skai Daniels."

"Nice to officially meet you. I'm a new fellow here. Just transferred from Johns Hopkins in–"

"Baltimore, yeah."

"Right."

"What made you leave Baltimore's program and come here?"

"My fiancé is an anesthesiologist here. Dr. Malik Harrison, you know him, right?"

My eyes shot down to her left hand, and there was, in fact, the same ring I'd found in Malik's apartment sitting pretty on her ring finger. *Fuck*, I grumbled to myself. I'd walked right into her trap.

"Y–yeah. I know him."

"I was hoping we could talk. Hence, the coffee that you still haven't taken out of my hand."

"Oh, I'm sorry. Um, thank you," I gulped, shifting the warm cup from her hand to mine, "but um, what would you and I have to talk about?"

"Well, we could start with the elevator back there; that was weird, right? It wasn't just me?"

Heart pounding, I frowned. "W–what do you mean?"

She shifted her weight from one leg to the other. "Listen, we can pussyfoot around the obvious all day if you want, or we can sit down as women and have a real conversation."

"Can't promise I'll be much fun. I'm not the chatty type."

"I'm sure you're underestimating yourself."

"Listen, now's not the best time, okay? I have to get my patient prepped for surgery," I blurted out before spinning my heels in the opposite direction.

"Mrs. Bowles in 4131?" she called out.

"Y–yeah. H–how'd you–?"

"I'll be scrubbing in on that surgery today as well," she informed me with a smirk across her face.

I huffed. "Oh. Okay. Fine, let's talk."

The two of us stepped into an unoccupied exam room, and she closed the door behind her. "I know about you and Malik."

My brow creased. "Excuse me? There's nothing to know."

"Let me be very clear. I know you were *fucking* him."

The way she let the f-bomb roll off her tongue made me turn and look her directly in her chocolate brown eyes. Embarrassed, I knew my cheeks had taken on the hue of wild cherries. I sighed. "Listen, Nichelle–"

She held her hand up to stop me. "No, you listen. I've been here for a week, and it's the same energy shift whenever you enter the room or elevator in today's instance. He sees you walking down the corridor, and he turns the other way. He sees you in line in the cafeteria and insists we go somewhere off campus to grab a bite to eat. I've been in the room with other girls he's fucked before, Skai. You're different."

I shot up a questioning brow. "What makes me so different?"

"Trust me, I've been trying to figure that out since I got here. I'm marrying him, but I know some of him will always belong to the streets, to you even."

"Then, why go through with it?" I asked, knowing I was likely overstepping.

Her shoulders rose and fell in a lazy shrug. "I love him."

"And that's enough for you?"

"Some days it is, some days it's not. He's flawed. I know that. At least I know what he's doing and when he's doing it. He respects me enough not to play in my face, y'know? And although I came here for him, my career is still very important to me, and if I'm going to walk in here every day and try my best to thrive here, then I need to know if you're still fucking my fiancé."

My eyebrows shot up. Malik may have been my last fuck, but he'd surely been the last thing on my mind with everything that had gone down. "N–no. It's done. It's been done. It was off and on at a point, but it's–there's nothing."

"And you're sure?"

"Yes," I answered.

She let out a long sigh as if she'd been holding her breath, awaiting my response. "Okay then. Thank you for your honesty."

"So, where does this leave us? Are we going to have a problem?"

"No. I'm a professional. Whatever happens outside of these walls gets handled out there."

I nodded as my feet paced to the door. "Okay then. Cool."

"And Skai?"

"Yeah?"

"Just so we're clear, I'm here now, and I'm here to stay. So make sure the *'nothing'* between you two stays that way. For good this time."

After a hellish work shift, I sat inside the darkness of my car and ripped open the envelope Bankx had given me to count how much money was inside. My eyes bugged as I realized hundreds of big faces were staring back at me, equaling out to ten thousand dollars.

"Oh shit," I muttered.

I didn't know how he'd gotten it or what he had to do to get it, but if it belonged to Jade, the least I could do was take it to Ba and make sure her family had what they needed. I pulled into the shopping center where her family's nail shop was located to see Ba locking up and pulling the metal gate down over the door for extra security. After putting the car in park, I hopped out and called out to him.

"Hello, Mr. Tran."

He turned to me with sad eyes. "We're closed."

"Oh, I know. I don't want my nails done. I'm Skai, Jade's friend."

His face lit up for a split second at the mention of his daughter's name. "She's not here," he responded, head low.

I drew in a deep breath and slowly exhaled. "I know. We—we only met a handful of times, but I just wanted to come and pay my respects, and um, to—to give you this, to help with her memorial expenses or anything else you may need," I implied, offering up the overstuffed envelope to him.

He looked down at the envelope and then up at me. "I don't want your money."

"No, it's not my money. It's Jade's."

He stared at the envelope a while longer as if he needed more convincing, so I spoke up again. "She, um, she had me hold onto it for emergencies, y'know, like a rainy day fund. And now that—that she's um. I just felt like you should have it. So, please, please take it."

He reached out for the envelope and looked inside. "All of this was hers?"

"All of it," I answered.

He dipped his chin. "Thank you for bringing this to me, Skai. I know Jade was very fond of you."

"So, you do remember me?"

"It has been a while since I've seen you, and these eyes aren't getting any younger, but yes, I recalled your voice once you began to speak."

"I'm sorry it's taken me so long to come over. I'm just–I'm still not okay about all of it," I confessed.

I decided it was best to spare him the details about how nothing smelled, tasted, or felt the same since Jade died. If anyone felt my pain, I knew he did.

"Are you hungry?" he asked, "we are having relatives and friends visit my home tonight. There will be all of Jade's favorite Vietnamese dishes and an altar with photos of her, and then tomorrow, in traditional Vietnamese Buddhist customs, we will cremate her body."

I looked down at the scrubs I had on and fiercely shook my head. "I'm not dressed; I–I couldn't–"

"Come to my home, Skai. It would mean a lot to Jade if you were there to show your respects. It may also help you find peace."

Knowing I couldn't say no, I nodded. "Okay."

From beginning to end, Jade's funeral was a three-day process. Things still hadn't fully sunk in when day three rolled around. I wasn't ready to say my final goodbyes. Aside from my estranged relationship with my father, Jade was the only family I had. As a physician, I knew death would come to collect us all one day, but I couldn't shake the shit. I had so much rage and guilt for leaving her to die alone and in pain that some days, it had me ready to hang everything up.

Her final service was a truly beautiful yet somber occasion. There wasn't enough waterproof mascara or eyeliner in the world to withstand my tears. Dressed in white, I stood on the shore with her relatives, each of us holding Jade's favorite flower, purple orchids, in our hands. Monks chanted and prayed throughout the service as the waves crashed and roared in the background. After the service, I said my goodbyes to her relatives and started making my way out of the sand.

"That was a beautiful service back there," a male voice called out just as I approached the low, wooden bridge.

I twisted my neck to see a man dressed in a black button-up shirt that looked like it had been glued to his body and matching black slacks. "Do I know you?" I replied, dabbing my eyes with fresh tissue before sliding my sunglasses over them to hide the puffy redness.

"No, you don't. But what if I told you I knew who did this to your friend?"

I scoffed. "I'd ask you why aren't they behind bars yet, since you know so much."

"Let me introduce myself. I'm Agent Miguel Martinez."

I suddenly paused. "Agent?"

"Yes and let me first say my condolences on the deceased."

I bobbed my head. "Thanks. It was nice meeting you, but I have to go."

"I was hoping you had a second to talk."

"I don't think we have anything to talk about," I asserted, head wagging from left to right.

"We could start with the fact that I know you were there that night."

My eyes sliced through him. "W–what?"

"I heard the recorded 9-1-1 call you made. I know you tried to save her life, Skai."

"Well, that doesn't make much difference now, does it?" I asked, swiping a tear from my cheek.

"I know now may not be the best time, so when you're ready to talk more about your friend and help me take down the sick bastard who murdered her in cold blood, you give me a call," he insisted, handing me his business card.

BABY

TWO DAYS LATER.

While waiting at a stoplight, I noticed something lodged between the passenger seat and the center console. I pulled it out to see Skai's face and name printed on her work nametag. She became the most prominent thing on my mind when I saw it. After taking a glance at my surroundings, I realized I wasn't too far from the hospital she worked at and decided to pull up on her and attempt to return it. I must've looped around the entire first floor three times before stopping to ask someone for help. Just as I was about to approach a receptionist, I saw Skai walking toward one of the patients' waiting areas.

"Dr. Skai Daniels?" I called out while jogging over to her.

She looked at me with apprehension on her face. "Ju?"

A smirk sprang to my lips. "Wassup, gorgeous?"

"What, um, what are you doing here?"

"I was in the neighborhood and shit. Figured I'd swing by, get an X-ray or somethin'," I joked.

She smirked. "Funny. Real funny."

"Nah, but for real. I brought you something," I informed her, reaching into my pocket to pull out her nametag. "I found it in the car and figured I'd return it."

She looked down at it and then back at me. "It's been over a week. You had to have known I'd get another one, right? Besides, losing or forgetting my nametag was kind of my thing around here when I was an intern."

I gave her a once-over while she talked. Although still beautiful, there was a cadaverous, empty look to her. Her bowed shoulders and the dark circles under her eyes told me she hadn't been getting the proper sleep. Her low curly ponytail was matted, and her eyes kept drifting focus.

"How you been?" I asked, head cocked to the side.

She shrugged. "I don't know. As good as to be expected, I guess. I mean, her funeral was a couple of days ago, so I'm still trying to process this whole thing."

"You sleeping?"

"Some. I've been staying overnights in the on-call room so I don't have to go home and sleep alone. It's that or hotels." She lowered her voice. "And to top it all off, he was here."

"Who?" She carved her eyes into mine, trying to tell me what she was trying to say without opening her mouth. "We can't talk about that here," I replied.

"I can't talk about it to anyone but you."

I sighed before stepping closer to her so no one would overhear our conversation. "What did he want?"

"He gave me...*ten thousand dollars*," she whispered, "said it was Jade's money, so I took it to her family."

"Hold up. He approached you? When was this?" I asked, noticing how her hands would shake ever so slightly whenever she talked about him.

"Last week. He hasn't been back since."

Hearing her confession and seeing how unwell she was made me uncomfortable. That should've been enough for me. It should've been all I needed to walk away and leave her right where she stood, but knowing she was scared made me want to protect her even more.

"I'm sorry she had to get you wrapped up in all of this."

"I'm sorry too."

"No need to apologize."

"Sorry. Force of habit," she admitted, glancing down at her jittery caffeinated hands.

"When was the last time you ate?"

"Haven't had much of an appetite outside of coffee."

"Let me feed you. Then, I'll let you go."

"I don't really have time to get away from the hospital."

"Isn't there a cafeteria or snack machine around this mothafucka or somethin'?" I chuckled.

Grin lines slashed her cheeks. "Uh, yeah. C'mon."

Skai led the way to the hospital cafeteria, where she grabbed a basket of fries and sat at an empty table.

"I know it hasn't been that long, but nothing feels right without her," she confessed, toying with the curly fry in her hand.

"It might not for a long time, but it will again."

"When?" she asked, casting doubt with a raised brow.

"One day."

"I'm a doctor. I see death every day, and I know loss. I should be able to handle this, but I'm completely cracking under the pressure."

"You feel helpless, right? Like a cowardly bystander watching as death comes for the person you love."

She nodded. "That's exactly how I feel."

"I ain't no doctor, but I know loss too. Lost my mom to cancer when I was younger."

"Really? At thirteen, I lost my mother to an incurable brain tumor."

"Damn. I'm sorry. I bet she was beautiful."

A smile pulled her mouth to one side. "Yeah, she was. She always wore her hair in these natural, individual twists and had this super deep dimple in her right cheek."

"That's where you get yours from, then."

"Yeah. Growing up, everyone said I looked like her, even though my father was white. We don't talk much these days."

"Yeah? Why not?"

She shrugged. "I don't know. I think he lost a part of himself after my mom died. He just wasn't the same. He didn't know how to raise a teenager by himself, let alone one that was half-Black. There were always questions I had that he couldn't answer, and I remember him getting so frustrated that I stopped asking altogether."

"Damn."

"What about you? Do you have a relationship with your dad?" she inquired.

"He got deported back to Jamaica when I was young. We talk here and there, and I fly out to see him every other Christmas. But to be honest, my brothers stepped in and stepped up once he left. It was like, yeah, okay, I may have lost my dad, but now I got two niggas in his place. So, it's like, I didn't really feel as much of a void, y'know?"

"Yeah. So, you're biracial, too, right?"

I dipped my chin. "Cuban and Jamaican."

"So, then you get it?"

"Get what?"

"How hard it is to fit in. Jade was the only person I could talk to about it. Not everybody gets stuff like that. In one crowd, I'm not Black enough. In others, I'm not white enough."

I nodded. "My mother's family never accepted any of us. We weren't Cuban enough to them just because our mother fucked around and fell in love with a Rasta. So, she disassociated herself from them. Her parents, sisters, brothers, everybody. We learned the Cuban culture through her, and she celebrated some of our father's traditions, even when he wasn't around."

"That's dope to have had a parent who understood the importance of teaching her children about all their history and not just keeping it one-sided."

After twenty more minutes of conversation and getting to know things about one another, she announced that her lunch break was over and that she had to get back to work.

"I'll walk you out," she insisted.

We were laughing and joking on our way out of the cafeteria when her energy shifted. I looked ahead to see a male and female doctor wearing white coats and holding hands, making their way toward us.

"What's the problem?" I asked, sensing the vibe switch.

"Nothing let's just ignore them," she insisted, dropping her gaze to the ground.

"Why?"

"No reason, just let's just not say anything t–"

"Hey, Dr. Daniels. Who's your friend? Or is this a patient?" the male doctor asked as they stopped a couple of feet in front of us.

"He's not a patient, Malik. This is Judah, my, um–"

"Her man."

"Your man?" he asked, making sole eye contact with her while his girl stood there looking stupid.

"That's what the man said, Malik. Let's eat. I'm hungry," the female doctor insisted.

Knowing the pretty boy in front of me had to have been an ex of hers, I tossed my arm around Skai's shoulder for good measure. "That's right. Get on to your meal, champ. C'mon, baby, let's go." I snickered while kissing her cheek.

The two of us walked off and turned the corner hand-in-hand before Skai jumped high with laughter sounding from the depths of her belly. "Oh my God! Thank you so much for having my back just then. You made my year, like seriously!"

I shrugged. "It was nothin'. Just felt like making a nigga mad."

"Did you see his face? Oh my God, it was priceless!" She cackled.

"Yeah, that nigga was super mad."

We approached the automatic sliding doors in the lobby. "Thanks," she stated warmly.

"For what?"

"Y'know, forcing me to eat, swooping in, and saving the day with that asshole back there."

"Don't mention it. What are you doing this weekend? Any plans?"

"I'm not sure. I have the entire weekend off. Even with the time off I took recently, I'm usually over eighty hours at the end of the work week. My chief resident said he will have to send me home more often."

"So, you've got the entire weekend off, and nothing to do is what I'm hearing."

She shrugged. "Pretty much. A part of me feels like I just need a reset, y'know? Like, I just wanna be on an island somewhere with zero responsibilities."

"Yeah?"

"Yeah, but enough about me. What about you? You got plans, or is the plan to be just as boring as me?"

"My brother's getting married this weekend."

"Oh, nice! Congratulations! To him, of course. Not you." She chuckled.

"Yeah. You, uh, you should come."

"To the wedding?"

"Why not? You're off, and it's something to do. Plus, it'll get you out of the city, so you ain't lookin' over your shoulder."

"Wait, it's not local?"

"Nah. It's a destination wedding or whatever you call it."

"Where exactly is the destination?"

"Say yes first," I insisted.

"Say yes? What do you mean say yes? I can't just say yes with no background information."

"You said yes like three times just now. And I gave you the details. It's my brother's wedding, and you gon' be safe because you'll be with me. Plus, this is my way of keeping an eye on you and making sure you taking care of yourself."

"Oh, so *you're* the doctor now?"

"If that's what it takes."

"Tell me where the wedding is going to be."

"Say yes first."

She folded her arms across her chest and shifted her weight from one leg to the other. "Why are you being so stubborn?"

Why are *you* being so stubborn?" I asked.

"Hypothetically speaking, if I did say yes, what would the sleeping arrangements be?"

"You can have your own room."

"And bathroom?" she negotiated.

A huff of laughter escaped my nostrils. "Whatever you need."

"And this isn't weird for you?"

"Nah. You?"

"A little."

"We've slept under the same roof before, and you were fine, right?"

"Yeah. You're right."

"So, you gon' give me an answer or continue to leave me hanging?"

"Fine, okay. Give me your phone. I'll put my number in, and you can text me the details and let me know what I gotta do."

"You don't have to do anything but show up. I'll take care of the rest."

"Can you please tell me where we're going now?!" she demanded.

I smirked. "Jamaica."

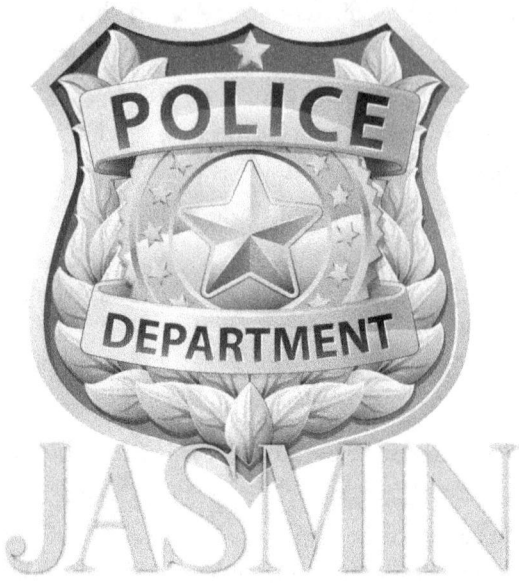

JASMIN

Bankx had spared no expense, wining and dining me across the city, yet I was no closer to getting a lead on his business dealings or his uncle's operations. I knew he was planning something big; I just didn't know what. The more I could get him to keep me around, the more opportunities I'd have to find out what I needed.

"You good?" he asked.

I glanced at him from the passenger seat of his pickup truck. "Yeah, why?"

"You're quieter than usual, like you got somethin' weighing on your mind."

"Maybe I do."

"What is it?"

I sighed. "I wanna tell you something, but I don't know how you're gonna react. Hell, I don't know how I'm gonna react."

"What is it?"

"I'm starting to fall for you, Jarrell. I think this could really be something between us."

"Yeah?"

"Mmhm."

Things fell silent for a few seconds before he spoke up again. "I think so too."

My ears perked up at the sound of his response. I'd finally made some headway. "I'm glad to hear that."

"Maybe now you'll consider spending the night."

"I didn't think you'd be the type to want anybody up under you for a full twenty-four hours," I joked.

"Not anybody but for you, I'll make the exception."

A smile curled the edge of my mouth. "Why me?"

"Why not you? You're my peace. I always need that with me, as long as you keep it honest with me."

"Well, okay then. I can do that."

"Good, and in return, anything you need, I got you. Just say the word," he announced.

My brow arched. "You got it like that?"

"You know I do. That's what your man is supposed to do."

"My man? Are we making things...y'know, official?" I quizzed, brow arched in his general direction.

"If that's what you want."

"It is, but only on one condition."

"And what condition is that?"

"You let me stand on my own two feet. We can be together, but I don't wanna rely on you for everything. I can pay my own bills."

"I thought you liked it when I spoiled you."

"I'm not saying you can't, but it's important to me that you know your money isn't all I care about. You know that, right?"

He nodded. "I do, and I admire the shit out of you for that."

"Why, thank you. Do you know what I admire about you?"

"What?"

"That you're about your business, you're refined, not sloppy. I can tell you know a lot about money and the streets. I just think it's all fascinating."

"Fascinating, huh? Trust me, baby girl, ain't shit fascinating about the streets. This shit is just one business transaction after another."

"Where are we going anyway?" I asked, changing the subject.

"We've got a private showing with my jeweler in thirty minutes. I thought you'd look nice with a fresh pair of diamonds in your ears."

He pulled into a parking spot on the side of the street, and just before he shut off the engine, his phone rang, and his uncle's name and number popped up on the screen before he pressed accept on his cellphone.

"It's me. Can we talk?" his uncle asked before Bankx could press the phone up to his ear.

He exited the running truck and connected his AirPods to ensure the highest amount of privacy he could get. As hard as it was to catch everything, I whipped out my phone and started to take notes and text them to Miguel.

"Just wanted you to know I'm about ready to make my next move on those Snow mothafuckas. At first, I wanted to pick them off one by one, but now, I just wanna end all three of their asses at once!" Bankx rumbled outside of the truck.

Hearing the name Snow struck a chord with me. *What did the three of them have to do with Bankx?* I hadn't seen or spoken to Baby in years, although there was a time when I thought I'd for sure become Mrs. Judah Snow. A lot of things had changed since then. I was a much different person at twenty-six than I was at seventeen. Even still, I'd done enough growing up to know that he deserved an explanation about how we ended, but I couldn't risk making contact and blowing my cover. At the end of the day, I wasn't after him and didn't plan to get him involved if I didn't have to.

SKAI

I ARRIVED AT THE AIRPORT TO MEET JU, PER HIS INSTRUCTIONS. HE'D taken the initiative to arrange everything since he'd invited me to tag along for the weekend. All I knew was that we were flying to Jamaica for his brother's wedding on Sunday. Outside of that, I had no expectations of how the flight would go, let alone the entire weekend.

My luggage wheels rolled across the floor when my phone started to ring. "Yes?" I answered for Ju.

"I see you."

I paused, shifting my neck from left to right. "And where exactly are you?"

"Right here," he teased, walking up to me from behind.

A relaxed smile stretched across my face when I saw him. "Hey."

"I see you made it."

"I did."

"You ready for your unplugged weekend?"

"As ready as I'll ever be, I suppose," I answered with a shrug.

"C'mon, let's go."

I rolled my carry-on through the terminal, trailing a few steps behind him. It didn't take me long to realize we were flying private. I could get used to not worrying about people bumping into me and running their clunky luggage wheels over my feet, sifting through the chaotic sea of airport passengers, or taking off my shoes at the security checkpoint. Unbeknownst to him, I already felt spoiled, and I hadn't even laid eyes on the plane.

"There she is," he emphasized, pointing out to the runway.

I snapped out of my thoughts to focus my eyes on a white jet with the staircase down. "This is what we're flying in?" I asked, eyes bugged.

He ushered a nonchalant dip of his chin. "Yup."

"I thought this type of shit was only for like celebrities. I'm in awe, and we haven't even stepped inside."

"Gianna wanted the whole wedding party to travel together, and when it comes to her, whatever wifey wants, wifey gets as far as my brother's concerned."

"Gianna is the bride, right?"

"Yeah. Don't worry; I'll introduce you to everybody."

"Everybody?" I paused. "How many people are going to be on the–"

"Relax and c'mon. You'll see."

I followed Ju up the stairs and onto the jet to see seven unfamiliar faces staring back at me. "It's about time you got here," a man dressed in all white, who I assumed to be the groom, said.

"Yeah, we were about to have the pilot leave your ass, nigga," another male added.

"Shut up. You niggas know I like to make a grand entrance and shit," Ju responded.

"Wouldn't be you if you didn't," the bride joked. She matched her husband-to-be with all-white attire, and a miniature veil pushed to the back of her head.

"Everybody, this is Skai. Skai, this is everybody. My brother, Chief, his soon-to-be wifey, Gianna, and my niece, Dream. My brother Rome, his lady Lira, Gianna's best friend, Tony, and her cousin, Maya."

I waved with a teeth-flashing smile. "Hi, everybody. Nice to meet you all, and congratulations to the happy couple."

"C'mon, I'll show you around," Ju motioned with a wave of his hand.

Everything about the private jet was like something out of a movie. There were dozens of cushioned butterscotch-colored leather seats that reclined, a dining room table with seating for six, an office, bedroom, bathrooms, and an entertainment area. It was the pinnacle of luxury travel.

"You like it?" Ju asked after giving me a tour.

"Like it?! This is beyond nice! I've never flown first-class before, let alone chartered a private jet anywhere. You've completely ruined commercial flights for me. Like, this is some next-level, boss shit and something I could get used to."

"Thought drug dealers weren't your type," he quipped, throwing my past comments back in my face.

"Both things can be true," I replied with a smirk.

I couldn't believe I was on a plane with a practical stranger and his family. Yet, it was the most comfortable I'd felt since losing Jade. He was right, though, I had made it painfully clear that drug dealers weren't my thing when we first met, but I wasn't above changing my mind for the right person.

By the time we ascended into the air, my head was already in the clouds, and they made sure I knew they planned to keep it that way until we landed.

"Alright, beautiful people! It's game time!" Gianna announced with a deck of cards in her hand.

"What kind of game?" Chief asked.

"Truth or dare, bae!"

"Truth or dare, girl? What grade are we in?" Gianna's cousin, Maya, asked.

"Truth is for pussies!" Ju yelled out, laughing as he spoke.

"That's why I have some of my own rules. Anytime anyone picks truth, they gotta take a shot."

"How you gon' drink when you pregnant?" Lira asked.

"Chief will take my shots for me!"

"Shit, I'm picking truth to get drunk then," Rome joked.

"Everybody down?" Gianna asked.

"I'm in," Gianna's friend, Tony, added.

"We're in, too," Lira spoke up for her and Rome.

"Fuck it, why not?" Ju added. "You playin', Skai?"

"Yeah, I'll play," I agreed.

We started to move around the circle in a clockwise direction, each picking either truth or dare and pulling a card from their respective piles.

"Alright, Maya, it's your turn. And don't forget to read the question aloud," Gianna reminded her cousin before she plucked her card.

"Fine, okay. I picked truth, and the card says, what color panties are you wearing," she whined before covering her eyes with the small card.

"You have to answer it!"

"Plus, take a shot!" I chimed in.

"I don't wear panties, y'all," she confessed.

Everyone roared with laughter, and a couple more truth cards were pulled, revealing who amongst the group had ever faked an orgasm or filmed a sex tape.

"Okay, Skai. It's your turn," Gianna announced. "Pick your poison!"

"Since I'm already buzzed off this strong ass Jamaican rum y'all got, I'm gonna play it safe and go with a truth," I stated, plucking a card. After quickly scanning my eyes over the card, I spoke up. "Okay, it says, if you could only ever do *one* position for the rest of your life, which one would it be and why?"

Ju looked at me, head tilted with a smirk across his face. "I'm interested in hearing this answer."

I giggled. "Oh, I bet you are! But, um, I'd have to say…missionary. And before y'all call me wack or old-school or whatever, hear me out! With the right person, there's a lot you can do in that position, spots you can hit that may not feel as good in other positions or go as deep, y'know? Plus, you get the intimacy of eye contact. Cheek to cheek, chest to chest, that's sexy!" I confessed, fully expecting to get clowned.

"I'm with you on that," Gianna added.

"Hell yeah. Let a nigga wrap his hand around your throat just right, have a bitch screaming!" Lira joked.

"Aight, aight, aight. It's my turn now," Ju announced, "and since all y'all are acting scary, I choose dare," he boasted, pulling a card from the pile and reading it to himself. "I'm not doing that shit, man."

"What it say?" Chief asked while taking a swig of the Jamaican rum in his cup.

"You have to do it! If not, then the group has to come up with an even worse dare for you to do!" Gianna stated, adding in a new rule.

"It says I gotta drop an ice cube down my pants. I'm not doing that shit," he protested.

"I think Skai should do it," Lira added before burying her nose in her glass, trying to avoid looking like the generator of the idea.

"Either that, or take two shots, plus you gotta pick another card!" Gianna proposed.

"Fine, fuck it. I'll take however many shots, and I'll pick another card."

We all watched him toss back two shots of Casa Migos tequila as if they were straight water before pulling another card from the top of the stack. "This one is worse than the last one!"

"What's it say?" Rome inquired.

"Make fuckin' eye contact with the mothafucka to your right and moan for *ten* seconds."

"Oop, that's Skai to his right." Lira giggled.

"That should be easy. Why you can't do that?" Rome pressed him.

"Nigga, I don't moan! I make the moaning happen, aight?"

Rome shook his head. "Nah, you just don't wanna embarrass yourself in front of your girl."

"She's not my–"

"I'm not his–"

We both stopped as everyone but us laughed at our expense for speaking at the same time.

"We're not together," I confirmed.

"*Yet*," Gianna added.

THE NIGHT BEFORE THE WEDDING.

I stepped off the plane Friday night wanting to know everything about Skai, from her favorite color to what things made a smile take possession of her lips. I hadn't felt that way or been interested enough in anyone enough to want to get to know them since I was a teenager. It didn't help that my brothers and their girls seemed to like her, too. Chief and Gianna rented a fourteen-acre private estate with twelve bedrooms and eight bathrooms to host the entire wedding party for the weekend and have their wedding on the property on Sunday. After continuing to party into the blue of the morning once we landed on Friday, I made sure to give Skai her space to reset and clear her head from all the craziness in Miami, for most of the day on Saturday. It wasn't until I'd finished getting dressed for the rehearsal dinner that I made my way across the hall to her room. Her door swung open, and she greeted me with a warm smile.

I stepped back to strike a pose, clad in a black, silk-collared button-up, dress pants, and tie. "How do I look?"

She reached out to straighten my tie before flashing her eyes up to mine. "Now, you're perfect."

"You sure you don't wanna come?"

"Nah. You enjoy your family. I'll be okay. I'm just gonna continue to kick back and relax.

"Got a lil' taste of solitude, and now you're hooked, huh?"

"Oh my God, it's like I knew I needed it, but I didn't know how much I needed the time and space to myself."

Before I could reply, my phone started to ring. I glanced down at the screen and knew it was a call I had to take. "I gotta take this, but I'll catch up with you later, okay?"

"Okay. Sneak me some cake or something if they have any."

I chuckled. "I got you." I swiped to answer the call while closing her door behind me. "Hello?"

I'd been on edge since the minute I got the call. After hanging up, I made my way through the gated property in search of Rome to relay the information that Giovanni had been killed when transported from one prison to another. We agreed that neither of us would say anything to Chief until after the wedding. Gianna's mother, father, and stepmother were already on the property, and I was hoping that word didn't get to them until they returned to the States. I was glad he'd been taken care of, especially after what he did to my niece, but I didn't want anything getting in the way of Chief's big day.

When I showed up to the rehearsal dinner without Skai by my side, I thought I'd never hear the end of it. The entire time, my brothers and their girls had been pushing me to admit I had feelings for her while their girls kept asking if we were together and teasing me about a relationship that didn't even exist. After dinner, I snagged Skai a piece of cake and headed back to her room to check on her like I said I would.

She answered the door wearing a two-piece loungewear set and some plush UGG slippers. "Hey."

"What's up? Thought you might be a lil' hungry."

"That depends."

"On?"

"What'd you bring me?" she inquired. The corners of her mouth lifted in a smile.

"Open the box and find out."

She opened it, and I watched her eyes flash with happiness. "Oh my God, cake! You brought me cake and a fork!"

"That's what you asked for, so yeah."

"Thank you! How was the rehearsal dinner and everything?"

"It was cool, but to be honest, them niggas were getting on my nerves."

"Why? What happened?" she asked, mid-bite.

"Everybody wouldn't stop talking about your ass!"

She broke into a short laugh. "Me? What about me?"

"Everything about you! Skai is so pretty. Is Skai your girl? Why'd you bring her if she's not your girl? Where is she at? Did you make her mad? We set an extra place for her!" I mimicked all the backlash I'd received.

"Oh my God! All that?"

"Yeah, you must've made a crazy ass impression on them on the plane ride."

"I like them all. They are so funny and laid back."

"What you doin' in here anyway?" I asked, leaning against the wall near her doorframe with one shoulder.

"Absolutely nothing."

"And how's that treating you?" I inquired.

"Quite well. I've been trying to fall asleep for forty-five minutes, but no luck."

"You want me to kick it with you until you fall asleep?"

"You asking me to hang out?"

"You got a problem with that?"

"Nope. Come in."

I walked into her room and pulled off my tie and button-up to get more comfortable before crashing down beside her on the bed. She'd placed a pillow between us, so I already knew what was up. "So, what's up? What you in here watching?"

"The TV has just been on. I told you I've been watching the inside of my eyelids, trying to fall asleep. Can you just talk to me until I knock out?" she suggested while rubbing her eyes sleepily.

"What you wanna talk about?"

"Anything. What's on your mind?"

"To be honest, you."

"What about me?"

I shrugged. "I don't know. This shit is wild, even for me."

"In what way?"

"Shit, everything. How we met, to you being here. It was unexpected, that's all. You make me not myself."

"I don't ever want you to not be yourself, especially around me."

"I'm not saying it's a bad thing, though."

"What do you mean?"

I shifted positions. "I don't know. I have this weird feeling when I'm around you. I can't explain it. All I know is it feels good. I know we haven't known each other that long or nothin' like that for anything I'm saying even to make sense. I don't know why my brain goes blank around you. I think I might be going crazy or somethin'. I just...adore the fuck outta you, Skai," I finished just before she shifted positions, stirring lightly.

"Skai?" I asked, eyes blazing down at her.

She'd fallen asleep, and a part of me was relieved she hadn't been conscious to hear my confession. My warm fingers stroked her cheek for a few seconds, gently tracing her features and counting the tiny freckles on the bridge of her nose as she slept peacefully next to me. Her eyelashes fluttered just before I heard her snore a little for the first time, making me chuckle.

"Goodnight," I whispered to her before closing my eyes.

SKAI

The wedding day.

I woke up to my legs draped over Ju's, relieved to see that we were both still fully clothed and on top of the covers. I watched him for a few seconds before slowly sitting up to inch over to the edge of the bed. Before my feet could hit the ground, his gravelly voice sounded off behind me.

"Good morning, sleepyhead."

I glanced over my right shoulder at him. "Me? I woke up before you."

"Because your ass passed out after three minutes of me being in here last night," he joked.

I flicked my hair out of my eyes. "I can't believe I fell asleep so fast."

"Yeah, your ass was out like a light."

"I dreamt you were talking to me when I was asleep."

"Yeah?"

I dipped my chin. "Yeah."

"What did I say?"

"I–I don't really know. All I remember is you saying something about how much you adore me or something about you going crazy."

His bushy eyebrows rose in surprise. "Wow, that's wild. I must've been trippin', huh," he replied with a lazy shrug.

"It's all a blur now anyway. I can hardly ever remember my dreams after I wake up."

"Yeah, me neither."

Our necks snapped toward the door when a loud banging sounded on the other side. I hopped up to open it, seeing a desperate bride and only one of her bridesmaids in tow, both with flexy rods in their hair to hold up their curls.

"Good, you're up!" Gianna declared with a sigh of relief.

"What's up?"

"I know you don't really know me, but I need you to do me the biggest favor of my life right now!"

Brows knitted, I asked, "What is it?"

"I need you to put on this dress and be my bridesmaid in four and a half hours. Lira, give her the dress!"

Lira shoved the garment bag with a dress inside into my arms. "Wait, what?"

"Yeah, hold up. What?" Ju asked, popping up behind me.

Gianna and Lira shared a look before putting their attention back on us. "Mmm, now we know what happened to him after the rehearsal dinner. Came over here for a lil' dessert." Lira snickered.

"Shut up, Lira. It ain't like that."

"What happened to your cousin? Her name was Maya, right?" I inquired.

"She had an allergic reaction to one of the appetizers last night. There was coconut in the shrimp, and she had to use her last EpiPen and everything, so she flew back to the States twenty minutes ago. Today is one of the biggest days of my life, and I'm freaking the fuck out right now, okay? I need you! I'll get on my knees and beg if I have to."

I shook my head firmly. "There's no need for all of that. I'd be happy to help you out. It's the least I can do for allowing me to come this weekend."

She pulled me into a tight hug. "Thank you so much! You're a fucking Godsend! Throw on something, and let's get you to the other side of the estate to start on hair and makeup!"

"Can I at least take a shower and then meet you, ladies over there?"

Gianna sighed while shaking her head. "I'm sorry. Of course, you can. I'll see you in a little."

I joined Gianna, Lira, and Dream in a separate cottage on the property used as the designated bridal suite. The view alone proved to be the most picturesque thing I'd ever seen, like something you'd see on a screensaver or tropical islands calendar but never in real life. The cottage alone was like its own boutique hotel with a pool outside that overlooked the ocean's turquoise waters.

"Thanks again for stepping up, Skai. It means more than you know," she said, optimism tinging her voice.

"You're welcome," I answered, sipping from my champagne glass. "This place is like heaven on earth."

Gianna's teeth flashed in a quick smile while sitting at the vanity in a white silk kimono as the makeup artist outlined her lips in crimson red paint. "It really is beautiful. Chief's father helped us find it. The moment I saw it, I knew it was perfect."

"I'm in love with everything. So much so that I wish I could pack the marble tub in my suitcase and bring it back with me," I joked.

"So, Gianna is a lot more poised than I am. I don't be giving a fuck sometimes, plus this champagne has me feeling a little loopy, so I just wanna know what's up with you and Baby," Lira inquired.

My nose wrinkled. "What do you mean?"

"You don't have to act all coy, Skai. Plus, we already caught you two practically naked in your room this morning."

A laugh broke through my lips. "No! You know damn well we both had on clothes!"

She cackled. "I know that, but it doesn't mean you ain't want that statement to be true."

"Um, yuck. Can we change the subject to something other than my uncle?" Dream interjected before the makeup artist outlined her cupid's bow.

Laughter rung out as we continued to get our makeup, nails, and hair done. "You feeling ready to walk down the aisle?" I asked, changing subjects.

"I can't believe the day is finally here. I mean, we had to do it sooner than later, I guess. I'm already twenty-one weeks along."

"I mean, I'm happy for y'all and everything, but real talk, I just can't wait for the cake!" Lira chimed in.

Dream bobbed her head. "Gianna does make some *bomb ass* cake."

Gianna grinned from ear to ear. "Why, thank you!"

"Know what you're having?" I quizzed with a smile.

"A bouncing baby boy," she answered, gently brushing her hand against her belly.

"Hashtag, boy mom!" Lira cheered in the background.

"Got a name picked out?"

"Not yet. I like the name Lucas, but Chief doesn't."

"I second that," Dream piped up. "I keep telling them the baby's name needs to start with a D like my dad and me."

"He says he doesn't want a junior, so the verdict is still out."

We turned our attention to the knock on the door before two female maids walked in to deliver a bouquet of roses to Gianna, Lira, and Dream. They were so dark red that they appeared black, but were beautiful, nonetheless.

"This has Chief written all over it. Roses are his thing. My baby is so sweet, y'all."

"What's the card say?" I asked.

Gianna reached out to grab the card, and her brow creased after reading it.

"Well, what's it say?" Lira asked.

"It's a bible verse..."

"A what? I ain't know that nigga read the bible," Lira joked.

"Shut up!"

"What's it say?" I asked.

"Deuteronomy 32:35."

"And that's it?"

"Yeah."

"That's poetic, I guess. Cryptic as hell, but poetic," Lira replied.

"What about the other cards?" I inquired.

Dream and Lira grabbed the cards from their bouquets, which revealed bible verses 1 John 1:8 and Psalms 144.

"What do all of these verses mean?"

"I'll look it up," I volunteered, pulling out my phone as the stylist put wand curls in my hair.

After reading each verse, I looked up at them with an uneasy feeling in the pit of my stomach.

"What? What do they mean?" Lira probed.

I gave Gianna and Lira a look that told them I couldn't say what I wanted to in the company of makeup artists and more, and they quickly cleared the room until it was just the three of us and Dream left.

Lira stood next to me. "What the fuck do those cards mean, Skai? I don't like the look on your face."

I drew in a deep breath. "Dream, your card had 1 John 1:8, right?"

"Yeah."

"It says, if we claim to be without sin, then we deceive ourselves, and the truth is not in us."

"What the hell does that mean?"

"Lira, your card was Psalms 144. It says, praise be to the Lord my rock, who trains my hands for war, my fingers for battle...."

"What?" she quizzed.

Gianna eyed me closely. "And what about mine? Mine was Deuteronomy 32:35."

I swallowed hard. "It–it says, it is mine to avenge; I will repay. In due time their foot will slip; their day of disaster is near, and their doom rushes upon them."

All the air left her body as she hunched over, holding her stomach. "No. No. Not here. Not today!" she sniffled. "It's nothing. It's probably just someone trying to scare us!"

"In Jamaica? No. I don't like this shit, Gianna," Lira protested.

"It's nothing, Lira. It's nothing. It's nothing. *It's nothing*," she chanted.

"I'm calling Rome."

"No, wait!" Gianna yelled. "We can't tell the guys. You hear me? Not today. You know them! They'll go to war, and this entire day will go out of the window. I don't want my wedding day to be marked with bloodshed, okay? Please let Chief and I have this day, and I promise we can tell them all tomorrow."

Lira stared at her hesitantly before her eyes shifted to Dream and me. "Gianna…"

"Please?"

She quickly dipped her chin. "The minute you two mothafuckas say I do, I'm telling him."

"Oh my God," I spoke up, cheeks losing their color when I remembered where I'd seen one of the Bible verses before.

I could feel a swirl of nervous knots in my stomach as my mouth hung open in disbelief. I dropped the cards to the floor.

"What is it?" Dream asked.

"I–I know where I've seen that verse on your card before, Lira."

"My card? Where?"

My chest rattled as I drew in a shaky breath, trying to form my words carefully.

"Bankx. It's Bankx!"

"How do you know that name?" Lira inquired.

"His tattoo! He has Psalms 144 tattooed on his forearm."

"You need to tell us how the fuck you know that name, and you need to tell us right now," Lira warned.

"He killed my best friend," I explained.

Her dark-arched eyebrows rose and fell. "He–he did what?"

"It's a long story and not one that's going to lighten the mood here, but–she used to dance down at his club. She did some extra work for him, and um, things went left, and he slit her throat and left her to die in an alley."

Gianna reached out to comfort me. "I'm so sorry."

"Thanks, but wait, y–you know him, too, Lira?"

She shook her head. "I never met Bankx personally, but I used to date his brother, Jevan. He said that Bankx had big plans for not just Rome but all three of them when he got out. Shit has been quiet for too long, and now he wanna strike?"

"Gianna, you need to tell my dad," Dream demanded.

"Dream, please–I can't have you here listening to this."

"I'm not going anywhere, Gianna. This involves my father and my uncles! I'm staying!"

I closed my eyes, unable to shake the chill crawling up my spine. Suddenly, my mouth was filled with a sour taste as if I'd licked a copper penny, and my stomach began to rock back and forth like a tugboat in the middle of a raging storm.

"I think I'm gonna be sick."

Lira ripped my phone out of my hand and handed it to Gianna. "Call Chief right now."

The suite was filled with the entire wedding party trying to decipher Bankx's cryptic messages in seconds. Lira, Tony, Dream, and I sat near Gianna, trying to provide her as much comfort as we could while Ju and his brothers deliberated.

"What you wanna do? Call it off?" Rome asked Chief.

"No. This is my fuckin' wedding day. Beef up security, do whatever we have to do."

"Fuck it, why don't we get married right now?"

"Right now?!" Gianna exclaimed. "Is everyone here?"

"The people that matter are. Your parents, our father, all of us, and the officiant."

"He's right, Gi," Tony assured her.

"Let's speed it up just in case he is planning something for the wedding. Just fill in the empty seats with the maids and chefs and shit. I don't care. All I wanna do is marry you, baby. That's all I give a fuck about today. Not that nigga, Bankx, or some other shit. I ain't gon' let that nigga win," Chief stated, standing his ground.

Gianna quickly nodded. "Okay. It looks like we're having a wedding right now."

I put on the dress, the heels, and a smile, defying the bad feeling nipping at my gut. I kept telling myself we were in Jamaica and far away from Miami. He couldn't get us. He *wouldn't* get us. Ju was already slated to walk down the aisle with his niece, Dream, which meant I had to walk down with Gianna's bestie, Tony. The two of us strutted down the aisle arm in arm. When my eyes locked on Ju's, I couldn't steer them elsewhere. His jaw was clenched, and his fists were balled tight, yet his eyes were soft when looking into mine. Just before we reached the end of the aisle, Ju made a funny face at me. I mouthed the words *stop it* to him before standing at Lira's side. It was then that I released the breath I didn't realize I'd been holding. I was happy to have his eyes off me, if only for a second. I couldn't think or breathe with him looking at me like that, yet I couldn't tear my attention away from him.

Surrounded by lush tropical greenery and turquoise waters, everyone stood in awe as Gianna, and her father marched over the ivy-covered bridge and headed down the aisle to Beyonce's *Dangerously In Love*. The private beach provided the perfect backdrop for their nuptials as Chief reached out to take her by the hand. The officiant began, and before I knew it, we'd gotten to the vows portion of the ceremony with Gianna speaking first.

Her voice cracked. "Chief, I stand before you today, a happy, complete woman. Everything I've asked for, you've provided. Everything I've needed, you've delivered. I feel like I've been in love with you for so long that I can't not love you. It's just not in me. You're my family. My world. My soulmate. My everything, and I can't imagine my life without you in it."

Chief wiped a tear from her cheek before parting his lips to speak. "Gianna, I didn't think I'd be doing this again. I promised myself I'd never get married again, and yet, all I've been thinking about since we landed on this island was, damn, I can't believe I get to marry her. I know today may not have turned out to be exactly what you expected, but you've still managed to take my breath away. You're a bright spark in a dark world, and I can't imagine a day without you, nor would I want to. I love you today, tomorrow, and forever," he proclaimed before leaning down to kiss her hairline.

After the officiant announced them as husband and wife, he pulled her in for a passionate kiss, both all smiles. The moment the officiant announced Chief and Gianna as husband and wife, he pulled her in for a passionate kiss before they turned to face us and their small gathering of guests, grinning from ear to ear. The place erupted with applause just as two women dressed as maids with dark shades over their eyes stood up and started spraying bullets everywhere. Screams rang out as bodies hit the ground, searching for anything to shield us from the shells. When the shots stopped ringing out, everything fell silent to where you could only hear the dull roar of the ocean in the distance. Seconds later, the screaming ensued again.

"Chief?! Chief?!" Gianna yelled. "Oh my God, he's hit! He got hit! We need help!"

Everyone raced to his aid, including me. Lira called the paramedics while I crouched beside him to assess the damage. His blood was bright red, like vermilion, which meant he was likely bleeding from an artery. "He's losing a lot of blood. How far away is the ambulance?"

"I–I don't know! They said they were on the way," Lira stated in a panic.

"Hold him down."

"What?" Ju asked, brows raised with concern.

"We have to stop the bleeding, or he'll bleed out before the paramedics get here. If you don't want your brother to die, I need you both to hold him down!"

"What do you need?" Tony asked.

"Alcohol and tweezers. He may go unconscious, but it'll get infected if left unattended."

Rome and Ju stood at their brother's side and held Chief's shoulders so he couldn't move while Tony raced to find everything I needed to try and save Chief's life. He returned minutes later with a half-open bottle of tequila and a pair of tweezers. I poured alcohol over my hands and the tweezers to sanitize them and dug inside his flesh to pull out the bullet lodged in his side.

Gianna got down beside him and placed his hand in hers. "I'm right here, baby. I'm not going anywhere, you hear me? I'm not leaving your side!"

"I'm here, too, Daddy. I'm not going anywhere," Dream added.

"Just keep looking at Gianna. Yup, that's right. Eyes on your beautiful bride. I know it hurts, but you're gonna be okay. We just gotta get the bullet out and see if we can stop the bleeding, okay? I'm almost done. Just keep your eyes on Gianna, okay? Focus on my words. Stay with me."

Chief pulled his clenched lips between his teeth before squeezing his eyes shut and

groaning. Tears leaked out the sides of his eyes, and beads of sweat populated his forehead. "Ahhhhhhhh!" he screamed.

"Almost got it. Just keep breathing."

I managed to get the bullet out and apply pressure to the wound until the paramedics arrived. Gianna raced to the hospital with him, unwilling to leave his side. Once the ambulance was gone, Ju and Rome wasted no time jumping into action. Everyone was crying and fussing, all of us trapped in a whirlwind of emotions and fear. Bankx had successfully stirred up a storm and hid in the dust, making his point crystal clear. He was gunning for us all.

BANKX

Far away from the safety of the shore, Bevin and I were spending time on a yacht, surrounded by hundreds and hundreds of miles of salty ocean water. After deciding to make things official, we spent much more time together. Beauty aside, we seemed to be highly compatible. I hadn't felt sparks like that with someone before. If she was going to stick around, I knew I needed to have a private investigator look into her. I'd always been the reserved, private type, and putting my trust in someone wasn't my nature.

The thirty-foot yacht pushed through the water, bobbing against the waves. I glanced up at the cloudless blue skies above us, feeling a cool breeze coming off the water as I sauntered up behind her and wrapped my arms around her slim waist from behind. "You've got goosebumps on your shoulders."

"Huh?" she asked, twisting her neck to me.

I rubbed her bare arms. "I said, you've got goosebumps on your shoulders. What's on your mind?"

Cradled in my grasp, she shrugged. "Nothing. Getting lost in thought a lot is kind of my thing. Sometimes, I think I live in my head more than the present."

"Yeah? What you be thinking about?"

"Different things."

"Like what? Be real with me. Tell me something about yourself."

"What do you wanna know?"

"Anything you wanna tell me."

"Well, I took piano lessons in the fifth grade and quit after my fourth lesson. I've read all the Harry Potter books twice, and I believe they are infinitely better than the movies. The Tom and Jerry Show has been my favorite cartoon since I was six, and it still is after all these years. I'm celibate; I haven't had sex in over nine and a half months. I'm sure there are hundreds of other things, but that's all I can think of right now," she revealed.

"Damn."

"What?"

"Nine and a half months is a long time," I joked.

"Says the man who works around pussy twenty-four-seven. I'm surprised you don't have a bunch of little ones running around down there."

I swung my head in a no. "Nah, no kids for me yet."

"N—nope," she stammered before clearing her throat, "no kids for me either."

"Y'know, neither of my siblings lived long enough to have kids."

"Well, what about you? Do you want any?"

I bobbed my head. "I wanna make sure I leave a legacy behind before my time comes to an end."

"You seem to talk about settling down, now kids. When do you see all that happening?"

"Soon," I assured her.

"Soon, like, the next few months or the next few years?"

I looked into her eyes. "You think you might be up for the task?"

"Maybe I am."

I let out a soft chuckle. "So, monogamy is something females still want these days, not just some shit they say?"

"It's not as uncommon as you think, at least not for me," she stated with a shrug.

Before a reply could pass my lips, my phone rang. "Hold that thought," I told her before stepping away to take the call.

After placing the phone up to my ear, I waited for the person on the other line to speak. "The hit went off as planned," she informed me.

It would've seemed morbid news that that should've cast a dark shadow over my day. Instead, a broad, Grinch-like smile spread across my face and amusement glinted in my eyes. "Good. Get on a plane and get back here. The other half of your payment will be waiting for you when you return," I stated before ending the call.

I returned to Bevin with two flutes and a bottle of champagne. "Good news?" she inquired.

I smirked, my delight ringing warm in my voice. "Why you ask that?"

"You're smiling," she said, noticing my teeth-bearing grin. "Plus, there's champagne," she mentioned.

"Well, then, yeah. It was great news."

"Mmm. Care to let me in on your little mental celebration?"

I tore my eyes away from hers to observe the beauty of the sky shifting to deeper shades of pink, purple, and orange, momentarily closing my eyes to soak up the last few rays of the sun before it sunk below the horizon. "The sun is setting perfectly, isn't it?"

She sucked her teeth before bumping her hip against mine. "You're so secretive."

I shrugged off her comment. "It's just in my nature. I'm a private, dominant, and demanding mothafucka. But who knows, maybe you'll change me," I suggested before popping the bottle of champagne.

I filled both glasses until the bubbles spilled over my hand and passed one to her. "Mmm. Maybe I will," she replied, raising her glass. "What are we toasting to?"

I clinked my glass against hers. "Victory."

SKAI

I WAS ABLE TO STABILIZE CHIEF'S WOUND UNTIL THE PARAMEDICS arrived. Gianna and Dream left in the ambulance with him while Rome and Ju wasted no time jumping into action. Within the hour, Rome and Lira had arranged to pick up their son and get back to Miami so they could lay low until they had a handle on the situation. Ju and I were back in Miami by midnight after ensuring everyone got out of Jamaica and back to the States. I stuck by his side like glue, waiting for an update on Chief's status. After stepping out of his shower and tossing on some clothes, I walked down the hallway to overhear the last bit of his phone conversation before he hung up.

"Was that Gianna?" I asked, joining him in the kitchen.

"Yeah."

"How is Chief? Is he okay?" I asked in a panic while toweling my damp hair.

"She said the hospital here couldn't give him the care he needed, so they airlifted him to Miami for emergency surgery. He's still in surgery, but she said he's expected to make it."

I let out a sigh of relief while holding my chest. "Oh, thank God! I'm so happy to hear that!"

"She said that if it weren't for you, he would've bled out before the ambulance arrived."

"I'm happy I could help," I assured him.

Ju closed the gap between us before gently swiping a piece of wet hair behind my ear. "I think you might be my good luck charm."

I tore my eyes down to the floor while shaking my head. "Don't say that. I've never been one to have much luck."

I glanced up to see his eyes carved into mine, and my frazzled mind immediately spun away from me. Suddenly, I was thinking about his stupid, kissable mouth and how I felt an electric jolt between my legs every time he looked at me.

"I'm serious. My brother would've been dead if it weren't for you. You saved his life, Skai. I can never thank you enough for something like that. We're all indebted to you. Whatever I gotta do to protect you, I will," he pledged, bringing his lips within the same breathing space as mine.

I didn't back away or flinch. "Y–you're welcome," I answered, eyes pinned on his lips.

Rather than waiting for him to make the first move, I draped my hands around his neck and fastened my lips onto his. I closed my eyes, envisioning myself melting into a puddle of liquid lust right on his marble floor. My breath hitched when he broke the kiss, lungs gasping out for air. I stared into his eyes, slickened with passion and lips gaped open.

"Don't look at me like that," I warned, desire spreading across my body. He just didn't know how wet I already was.

"Like what?"

"Like you can't wait to see me naked."

He swept his eyes up and down my body. "I can't lie. Your lips make a nigga wonder what the rest of you tastes like."

My heart hammered in my chest. "You can't say things like that to me."

"What you want me to say to you then?" he asked, pressing my back against the refrigerator.

Eyes glowing with lust, I replied, "Tell me goodnight. It's late. We should both get some rest."

His hands absorbed my honey-colored hips. "You sure?"

"Unless you had something else in mind?"

"I could think of a couple of things we could be doing right now," he made known, lips flirting with danger.

"Like what?"

Instead of responding, he allowed his lips to smother mine once again. Our tongues intertwined, speaking a language only they understood. Ju's strong hands slowly descended from the base of my neck to my waist. He paused there, eyes holding me hostage, before he took my delicate fingers in his hand and led me to his bedroom. He pushed me down onto his king bed and started to undress me, quickly removing my clothes and his before pivoting his warm, chiseled body against mine. Ju towered over me, touching my body as if his hands had known my curves for years, and it was the first time we'd connected. Our connection was electrifying and draining at the same time. I could feel his presence all over my body as if he had some sort of metaphysical hold on me.

He kissed from my chest to my stomach before submerging his head between my smooth thighs. As I watched him gently blow against my clit, my fingers quickly became entangled in his curls. My hips twitched with excitement, like a ticking time bomb seconds away from exploding. Ju's full lips sucked and nibbled at my clit before embedding his thick tongue deep inside my kitty, flipping and rolling his tongue like a fish out of water. He quickly flipped me over to place a trail of kisses against my bare back, starting from the tip of my spine to the top of my ass. He took turns gently nipping at my cheeks before spreading my pussy lips from the back and dipping his tongue inside.

"Mmm shit," I purred, nails clawing the sheets.

Baby snaked his long tongue into my slit, occasionally sliding his tongue up to my asshole before sticking his finger inside it. He was such a fuckin' poet, the way his tongue flipped and flicked over my juicy folds. Unable to string words together, I continued to moan and throw my ass back against his lips. I could barely control all the twitching and jerking my hips were doing as his warm tongue slid up and down my pussy like a Slip N' Slide in mid-summer. I was no match for his tongue's bold flicks and tender strokes against my sweet spot. Eyes clamped shut, I felt my first climax coming in waves. Valiant, spirited, spine-tingling waves.

"Oh my God, I'm fuckin' cummin, Baby! Baby, I'm cumming!" I squealed out, bucking harder against his lips.

"That pussy is a fuckin' ocean," he mumbled before kissing the top of my pussy.

"Mmm, shit. Let me ride it," I whispered to him, making him aware that I was more than ready to feel the dick I'd fantasized about for nights.

He laid back while I climbed on top of him, jacking his dick while rubbing on my nipples. I eased down on him slowly until all ten inches of his caramel dick were inside, filling me to the brim. Unsure if it was more pain than pleasure or the other way around, I gripped his sculpted, firm shoulders and held on tight. I eased up and down his girth, realizing Ju had the type of dick a bitch had to prep for with stretches and yoga poses.

"It's s–so big," I moaned.

He grabbed hold of my bare hips before sitting up to mash his lips against my neck and collarbone. My fingertips roamed over his back as his lips moved down to latch around my mocha-brown nipples. I bucked faster, rolling and thrusting my hips back and forth until I could feel myself about to peak.

"Oh–oh my G–God! Stick your fucking finger in my ass!" I urged him, voice almost savage.

He obliged. "Oh, you like that nasty shit, huh?"

"Mmm, yeah."

"Mmm, shit," he groaned before smacking my ass, "turn that ass over then."

I complied with haste as if he'd put a loaded gun to my head. Baby slid out of me long enough to spin me around. I could feel his eyes probing into me from behind when my hips flared out after he'd bent me over the bed. He brushed my hair to the side and kissed the top of my spine while burying himself back inside my warmth. He squeezed my breasts, thumbs circling my rock-hard nipples. My screams and moans filled the room with each deep, powerful thrust.

"Mmm, yes!" I moaned, gently sliding back and forth against his rod.

"Tell me how you want it."

I arched my bronzed back. "Deep! I want it deep, Baby!"

"Fuck, I'm gonna give it to you so deep," he promised, smacking my cheeks.

With his strong arms holding my dainty waist captive, Baby picked up the rhythm, slamming into me harder, faster, and so fuckin' deep. He fucked me mercilessly with long, deep strokes while his brazen hands twisted my arms behind my back like a pretzel.

"Yes! Yes! Oh my God! Yes!" I yelled, face buried in the sex-scented sheets.

"Mmm. That pussy is drippin'. She must like that shit."

"Loved that shit," I corrected him.

My legs trembled, threatening to collapse underneath me with each long, deep stroke. I knew I was minutes, if not seconds, away from tapping out.

Switching positions, Ju fused his body against mine. He allowed his erection to push past my walls while he claimed my lips with a passionate kiss, dipping his tongue in and out of my mouth. I secured my legs around his waist while my fingers ran amok through his Tarzan-style curls. Ju stroked my body like a violin with a burning desire in his eyes. I gently gnawed at the diamond sitting in his earlobe before meshing my lips against his neck.

"Tell me how good this dick feels," he whispered in my ear.

"Shit, it feels so good," I panted, lungs on fire.

He lifted my legs to the sky before wrapping his hand around my fiery hot throat. He pumped faster, sending us both into the quakes of a double orgasm. We collapsed against the bed, hips twitching in aftershocks and hearts pounding. Our sweat-slicked bodies lay in a euphoric paralysis, and before I knew it, I was out. His dick had lulled me to sleep like a lullaby.

BANKX

I SAT PERCHED INSIDE MY TRUCK, WAITING IN THE ARRIVALS SECTION AT the airport for my uncle, when my phone dinged with a text from an unknown number.

UNKNOWN:

He survived.

"Fuck!" I said powerlessly, slamming my phone into the passenger seat.

I was pissed as fuck after finding out that not only did the two female assassins I sent to kill all *three* brothers failed, but once I got word from the girls that the hit had been executed, I never heard from them again. Neither of them made it back from Jamaica. On top of that, their asses retaliated three days later with shooters of their own who shot up my fuckin' club. I was aware that I had to watch out for them, so I made sure to lay low after the hit but didn't expect them to shoot up my place of business. It was such a loud, public retaliation. I had to shut my doors to the public, which meant no drugs circling through the club and no money coming in. I had to press the contractors and pay some hefty fines to be able to reopen my doors in two weeks to get business back up and running like normal.

I didn't personally have beef with Chief, but those niggas got in the way of *my money,* and I *still* didn't have my fuckin' diamonds back. And leaving one brother alive to avenge the two I didn't fuck with wasn't a good idea in my book. Therefore, I wasn't going to be satisfied until all three of their asses were pushing up flowers.

"I gotta do this shit myself," I grumbled.

Although I'd done my time, I knew the Feds were still watching me. I was trying to keep my hands as clean as possible, letting the pawns I'd put in place do my work while I sat back and enjoyed the show, but some things had to be handled by me and only me. I put my thoughts aside when I saw my uncle pop through the automated glass doors. He called and said he was catching a late flight into Miami to discuss a new distribution plan. Several times, I tapped my fist against the horn and rolled down the window to flag him down. For a fifty-seven-year-old man, he still looked like he could be in his mid-to-late forties. All the money he collected on the daily had done him some good.

"What up, nephew?"

He put on his seatbelt, and I reached out to dap him up. "What up, Unc? You in the city kinda late, ain't you?"

He smoothed his hand down his gray-stubbed chin. "I do my best business after the sun goes down."

"I see. So, what's up? On the phone, you said you were flying in to discuss a new distro plan. What's wrong with what we got?"

He handed me his phone. "Here, put this address in your GPS."

I glanced at him for a second, wondering if he would acknowledge my initial question. When he didn't, I put the car in gear. "Where we going?"

"We got some unfinished business to handle."

The bell dinged against the glass door of the diner. I shuffled behind my uncle to the back of the dusty establishment, past the long counter with spaced-out stools, the rusty jukebox in the corner, and all the empty booths nestled against the wall, to a table that seated six. He took his seat at the head, and I, to his right.

I glanced around at the selection of condiments collected in the middle of the table—then to the fingerprint-smudged window ahead of me with a view of the parking lot, then to the waitress delivering fries and shakes to the booth of teenagers at the opposite side of the diner. "The fuck we doin' here?"

"I'm hungry. Do you mind?"

A waitress wearing a stained white apron approached us and laid two laminated menus on the table. "What can I get you two started with this evening?"

Unc looked down at the menu. "How's your patty melt?"

"That's one of our daily specials today, sir."

"I'll take that with some fries and a Diet Coke."

She jotted down his request on her notepad. "Got it. And for you, sir?" she asked, peering over her rectangular-framed glasses at me.

"I'm straight."

"Okay, then. I'll go ahead and get your order right in."

Once she was out of earshot, I turned my attention back to Unc with a lowered brow. "You gon' tell me what the hell is goin' on now?"

"We'll start when they get here."

"Who is they?"

The bell on the diner door chimed again, and I looked up to see all three Snow brothers making their way inside. I grimaced. "What the fuck are they doin' here?"

I pushed myself away from the table when they approached while Unc stayed seated. The real reason he'd come to Miami became clear. It wasn't to meet to discuss a new distribution plan for his drug routes; it was to get us in check for all the back and forth.

Unc held out his hands. "Gentlemen, please be seated."

"Yo, Big Rey, what the fuck is this nigga doin' here?" Rome asked.

I sucked my teeth. "You know exactly why the fuck I'm here, nigga. But I could ask the same about pretty boy over there."

"You shot up my wedding, mothafucka. That's exactly why I'm here," Chief stated, standing up from the table.

"Unc, I'm not sitting down with these niggas," I refused.

"I could've lost my wife and my unborn baby behind you, nigga. Not to mention the rest of our families! There's nothin' you can ever say to earn my respect. Nah, you gon' have to see me, one way or another," Chief threatened.

I clenched my fist in a tight ball, ready for whatever. "And what about my sister, nigga? Or you forgot about Jhene?"

"Jhene's blood ain't on our hands, nigga. We ain't send them shooters!" Baby piped up.

I cut my eyes at him. "And what about Jevan, then, huh? Who's blood his hands on?"

Unc slammed his fists on the table, and the space fell silent. "That's enough! No more fucking bloodshed! This organization can't afford it! I want to resolve this shit peacefully. Everybody walks outta here alive at the end of the night. Aight? But if any of you refuse to sit the fuck down and go with how I say this shit is gonna go, then you already know where I stand," he warned.

My uncle was the type of nigga to speak money first. Family and anything else always came after it, so I knew what he said to be true. If you didn't fall in line, you'd get cut down, no matter who you were. The four of us begrudgingly took our seats around the table before Unc spoke up again. "I understand my nephew is a delicate topic for your family."

"He shot up my brother's fuckin' wedding," Rome griped.

"But, shooting up my nephew's club in retaliation, where I do *my* business, that makes me have to get involved in your mess, and I hate a fuckin' mess. I had to make a special trip down here to talk to you knuckle-headed mothafuckas about your erratic behavior so that you don't burn my organization to the fucking ground over pride and pussy!"

"Tell that to your bitch-ass nephew!" Baby grumbled.

"Let that shit come out your mouth one more time, and I'll show you a bitch-ass," I warned him.

"No more war! The past is the past. Rome, I don't blame you for what happened to Jhene. Losing her was hard for us all."

Rome shook his head. "With all due respect, I know you say you want this to be over, and I hear you, but he's had years to plot and plan against my family and me for some shit we never had anything to do with. We ain't get you set up, and I didn't get Jhene killed. Do you know how many times I prayed those bullets hit me instead of her?"

Hearing him out only tacked more guilt to the ton I already carried. I loved my baby sister and would've done anything to protect her. I knew Rome's confession was sincere because I was the one who sent those shooters. After I got locked up, I heard that Rome and Baby were the reason I got picked up by the Feds. All the hate inside me wasn't doing shit but festering into one evil plan after the next until I decided to arrange a hit from behind bars and catch that nigga slippin'. I had no idea Jhene would be with him at the time or that she was inside the car when they shot it up. I was the only one who deserved to live with the guilt of Jhene's life being lost. It was a secret I vowed to take to my grave.

"And Jevan?" I asked, looking dead into his eyes.

He lowered his head. "That's on me. I'll take that."

"Consider your debts settled. From here on out, it all ends. Agreed?" he asked, eyeing the four of us.

The table fell silent again before we all silently nodded. "Now that that's out of the way, we can get down to more important business."

"And what's that?" Baby asked.

Unc twisted his neck from left to right, cracking both sides before he spoke. "The Feds are breathing down my neck. Niggas are getting picked up by the FBI and DEA getting questioned about me, and I hear they're offering some sweet deals for the right snitch, which puts all of our business in jeopardy."

"Anybody talkin'?" I asked.

"Not yet. These niggas exist to serve me and distribute my product, and I pay handsomely for their loyalty, but sometimes that's not enough."

"If they aren't snitching, then what are they doing?" Rome asked.

"They are jumping ship, taking their business elsewhere because of all the heat."

"Fuck 'em. More product for us," Baby added.

"More product isn't a problem, but I need to lay low for a while."

"Who's gonna be your go-to in the meantime?" Rome asked.

Instead of responding, Unc rotated his neck in my direction. "In my absence, my nephew will be the forerunner of my operation."

"What!" Baby yelled. "First, you make us agree to put the beef aside, and now you tellin' us we gotta work directly with this nigga? Nah. I'm not with that shit!"

"We may have agreed to squash the beef, but I don't trust him. He could be waiting to set us up. We don't know what he has up his sleeve or who's on his payroll!" Rome pointed out.

"My nephew has been in the game for a long time. He understands the business, and he understands what's a stake here."

"So do we, and we don't need a handler."

"Exactly," Baby agreed, "we've always worked straight through you."

"You'll continue to run your operation as you see fit, and he'll continue to push my product through the club. You'll just get your product through him instead of me. Everybody still wins. Nothing changes about that."

A teasing smile crossed my face. "Time to pledge your loyalty, nigga."

"At the end of the day, my operation is in the red right now.

There's the product that needs to be pushed so that we can all continue to put food on the table. Make no mistake, boys, this is the new distribution plan. No one leaves the table until everyone agrees," he confirmed.

We all reluctantly shook hands, bonding us together in the most uncomfortable way, but if we wanted to continue to eat, Unc made it clear that it was the *only* way.

SKAI

Any time not spent at the hospital was spent laying up underneath Judah Snow. I hadn't expected such an immaculate stroke game. Ju had me ready to quit my job and move in under his roof so I could be prepared to surrender the kitty at a moment's notice.

I would have, could have fucked him on a plane.

I should have, would have fucked him in the rain.

I would have fucked him without a care.

I would have fucked him anywhere.

As good as the D was, I was more than *dickmatized*. It had been weeks since Jamaica, and our connection was stronger than I anticipated, managing to withstand international waters and my busy work schedule. Over those weeks, I'd somehow allowed myself to fall for him completely, but I wasn't quite ready to tell him how I felt.

After spending hours walking around the mall, Ju and I had our arms full of shopping bags and had worked up an appetite for more than designer labels.

"I'm hungry as shit. Where you wanna eat at?"

I shrugged. "I think I'm kinda in the mood for some Chinese. Is that cool with you?"

"Sure."

We made our way to the food court and sat our bags down at an empty table when I heard whimpering and crying nearby. I looked around and spotted a little girl standing all alone a few feet away from our table. She looked no older than three and was scared out of her mind. Seeing no other adult in sight, I walked over to her.

"Hey, hey there. It's okay. Where's your mommy?" I asked in a calm tone. She continued to cry before clinging to my thigh for comfort. "C'mon, let's see if we can find your mommy."

Ju swiped up our bags and followed me to the security station. The officers made an announcement in every store and over the loudspeaker, alerting everyone in the mall that there was a missing child. We waited at the security station for twenty minutes before a woman ran up to the security desk in a panic.

"Oh my God! Thank you! Thank you so much for finding my baby! You don't know how worried I was! I swear I turned my back for one freaking second, and she was gone!" she exclaimed.

She outstretched her arms to the child. "Come to Mommy, sweetheart."

The little girl went to her, and the woman began kissing her forehead and assessing her to ensure she was physically alright. I watched as Ju stared her down the entire time, looking as if he wanted to say something but was trying his hardest not to. Then, mall security and the police intervened to verify that the child did belong to her before letting them walk off together.

"Yo, I'll be right back," Ju stated before jogging away to catch up to the woman and child.

I watched them exchange words from a distance, the little girl clinging to her mother's chest before she turned and stalked off in the opposite direction. He walked back to me, taking note of the confused look on my face.

"You good?"

"Yeah. Are you?" I asked, flipping his question back at him.

"I'm straight."

"Still wanna get that Chinese?"

He shook his head. "Nah. I ain't really got an appetite no more. You?" he asked.

"Nah, let's go. I've done enough shopping for one day anyway."

On the walk back to the car, I tried to shake the feeling that something was going on that I needed to know, but it wouldn't leave my body. Ju's engine began to purr at the click of a button.

"You wanna talk about it?" I blurted out, unable to stifle my suspicions any longer.

"Talk about what?"

"Whatever's on your mind."

"Ain't nothin' on my mind."

"Your energy switch says different."

"What are you talkin' about?"

"Everything was good until that woman showed up to claim that little girl. It was like; I don't know, you two have a history or something."

"We ain't got history," he confirmed.

"Then, what do you have?"

"You remember my neck tattoo you asked me about that time?"

My eyes widened. *That* was your ex?"

"Nah. Her cousin, Tierra."

"Oh. What happened between you and Jasmin anyway?" I inquired.

"Why does it matter?"

"It doesn't, but it kinda does at the same time. I mean, she was an important chapter in your life. You can't keep it all inside, y'know? Bottling it up won't do any good."

"I'm not."

"You should be able to talk about it if you want to."

"I don't."

"Oh. Okay, I guess."

The car fell silent, and I turned my attention from him to the sites zooming by outside the window. "She got pregnant when we were seventeen, and her family wanted her to get rid of it, but I wanted her to keep it," he replied, eyes focused on the road ahead.

I slowly swiveled my neck in his direction. "What did she end up doing?"

"She had him."

"You two have a son?"

"*Had.* He was born prematurely at twenty-three and a half weeks, so he had a lot of health issues. He couldn't breathe on his own, and his organs were starting to fail, so we unplugged him at two days old. We named him Elijah."

His confession made tears fill my eyes. I reached out and placed my hand on his thigh. "Ju, I'm so, so sorry you had to go through that. That either of you had to go through that at such a young age."

"Yeah, it was tough, but I figured we'd get through it together. I'd loved her since we were twelve, but shit didn't work out that way."

"What ended up happening after that?"

"After Elijah's funeral, she told me she needed space. Three days later, she disappeared. Her family's house went up for sale, and everything was gone. She even changed her number. It was like I had made everything up in my mind."

"She just up and moved with no explanation?"

If I hadn't been looking his way, I wouldn't have known he'd nodded since no other words fell from his lips. I noted his balled-up fist in his lap and that he'd refused to look me in the eye during the entire conversation. It was still an uncomfortable and painful subject for him.

"I don't remember a fight or a reason. All I know is that she disappeared. I had to run down on her cousin and press her for information. That's when I found out they'd picked up and moved to Texas."

"And you haven't seen or heard from her since?"

"Nah."

"How long has it been?"

"Nine, maybe ten years."

I reached out and gently placed my hand on his shoulder. "I know a sorry won't change what happened, but for what it's worth, I'm truly sorry."

"What you got to be sorry for?"

"Running into her cousin like that had to stir up a lot of unrepressed feelings for you."

"I'm good. That was a long time ago. I'm over that shit."

"Who told you that you have to be strong all the time? No one has a heart of stone. Not even you."

He shrugged me off. "Yeah, well. I shut everybody out after that."

"Everybody, huh?"

"Yeah. Don't take it personally. It's just easier that way."

"For them or you?" He cut his eyes at me, refusing to give me the answer I already knew to be true. "Mmhm. That's what I thought."

BABY

I sat across from Skai in the booth at the coffee shop down the street from the hospital where she worked, watching her wash down her sandwich with an iced tea.

"Guess what?"

"What?" she queried, mid-bite.

"I snagged you one of those white chocolate chip cookies you like," I told her.

She smirked. "Are you serious? How? She told me they were all out when I went up there."

"That's because I know how much you like them and how quickly you said they sell out, so I stopped by before I came to the hospital," I confirmed, sliding it across the table.

She looked down at it and then back up at me with the corners of her mouth lifted. "Who sent you?"

"What?"

"You heard me. Who sent you? You're making me too damn happy. Like, this has got to be fake."

"How I feel about you is far from fake."

"And how exactly do you feel about me?" she inquired.

I tore my eyes out the window when I saw a woman walk past. It was like seeing a ghost. It couldn't have been who I thought it was. "Excuse me. I'll be right back."

I hopped up from the table and darted out of the restaurant. My neck jerked left and right, searching for the ghost of a woman I thought I'd seen from the restaurant window. I took off to my left and turned the corner to spot the woman walking about ten steps ahead of me.

"Jas?" I called out, silently praying she didn't turn around.

She spun around, eyes searching for the voice that'd called out to her, eyes landing on mine soon enough. "Judah?" She squinted, hand shielding her chestnut brown eyes. "Oh my God, it is you!" she said in awe.

My heart skipped a beat upon watching her dash over to me, heels clicking and clacking against the pavement. Seeing Jasmin again after so many years turned my world on its axis. It'd been a decade since I'd seen her, but she still looked the same, even smelled the same. She'd grown another inch or two taller but had the same glowing wheat brown colored skin and a canopy of long lashes over her mink brown eyes. Her grown woman body was curvy; hour-glass waist flaring in all the right places, with long, obsidian black hair that ended just below her bra strap.

I tipped my chin. "Yeah."

"How long has it been?" she asked, baffled.

"A long time," I answered, tearing my eyes down to the debris skittering across the sidewalk.

"You look good. Same Judah, just grown up."

I glanced around uneasily. "Yeah. You too."

"Thanks."

Her eyes welled with tears as she tossed her arms around my neck. "I've missed you," she whispered in my ear.

I pulled away, ungluing our bodies to confront her. "What are you doing here? Last I checked, Texas was your new home."

"It's kind of a long story."

My eyebrows squeezed together. "All these years, and you still don't think you owe me an explanation?"

"You're right, I do. Can I at least buy you a coffee? For old times' sake? Or a drink if coffee isn't your thing?" she quizzed, arching a questioning brow.

"I'm kinda in the middle of somethin' right now."

"Maybe some other time then?"

I nodded. "Yeah. Sure."

"Take my number down," she spoke, eyeing my phone.

I put her number in my phone and sent her a quick text so she'd have mine before turning around to head back to the restaurant. To my surprise, Skai stood a few feet away from us, watching the entire thing. *Fuck*, I thought to myself.

I jogged toward her just as she turned to storm off in the opposite direction. "Skai, wait up!" I yelled out to her.

She kept a quickness in her stride, darting across the painted crosswalk in the middle of the street. I ran to her left side and grabbed her arm to slow her down. She snapped it out of my grasp.

"So, you mad at me?" I quizzed.

"I don't have time for games."

"Neither do I."

She kissed her teeth. "Could've fooled me. I know what I saw!"

"Look, I stepped out because I thought I saw an old friend. We talked for like two minutes, that's it."

She bunched her arms up against her chest. "An old friend, huh?"

I sighed. "It was Jasmin."

"Your ex, Jasmin?"

"Yeah."

She scoffed. "First, we run into her cousin at the mall, and now suddenly, she's back in town? That's convenient."

"I didn't ask her to come back," I grumbled.

"But you sure didn't waste your time welcoming her back."

"I already told you about my history with her. I don't know why she's back, and I don't give a fuck."

She exploded. "You're so full of shit!" I watched you put her

143

number in your phone, Ju! Come on; you wouldn't have taken her number if you weren't the least bit curious if something was still there between you two. Just admit it!"

"You talkin' like I'm taken, and I'm not. It was just a conversation. It was my first time seeing her in years."

Her eyes welled up. "E—excuse me?"

I shrugged, uncomfortable with the entire conversation. "I was under the impression you knew what this was."

"And I was under the impression you understood me better than to be spending all my time with you for nothing."

"I care about you, Skai, but you sound insecure as fuck right now. High school was a long time ago. She's old news. Anything we had between us is dead and gone."

She sighed. "Are you sure?"

"Yes."

"If you had to choose between Jasmin and me, who would you choose?"

I sucked my teeth. "C'mon now, Skai. Don't do this dumb shit. I'm not with the jealousy and the back and forth."

"Tell me."

"Fine! If I had to choose, I would choose you."

"Really?"

"Yeah, really. I'm standing here arguing with you in public, ain't I?"

She sighed, looking around at the people walking by. "Look, I think I just need some space. Y'know, some time to clear my head and refocus."

My brows heightened in surprise. "Space? Really? Word?"

She nodded without bothering to make eye contact with me. "Yeah. I just blew up on you in public. You got me out here looking crazy over you. This ain't me! I need time to recollect myself, get my shit together."

"Then, maybe you're right. Maybe we should cool out for a bit."

"Ju—"

"Nah. You want space, you got it," I replied before walking away.

BABY

I FLIPPED THE SWITCH TO ILLUMINATE THE KITCHEN BEFORE MAKING MY way to the cabinet to grab a glass and pour myself a drink. I stood at the counter in mid-pour when my phone vibrated against the countertop. I sat the bottle of D'Ussé down and picked up the phone to see a text from Jasmin.

JASMIN:

You up for that drink?

ME:

Havin' one right now at the crib.

JASMIN:

I could join you...y'know, to talk?

I stared at the screen for a few seconds, contemplating my response. I could hear Skai's voice in my head, saying how much I *wasn't* over her. A part of me wanted to prove to her and myself that I was. It had been

145

years, and I'd buried everything that'd happened between us so far down to the point where it didn't hurt to think about it because I never did. I sent her my address, and once she hit me back saying she was on the way, I tossed the phone on the couch.

Thirty minutes later, there was a knock on the door. When I opened it, Jasmin was standing on the other side with an apprehensive look on her face. My grip on the door handle became stronger. It was one thing to run into her on the street. It was another for her to be standing in my doorframe. A nagging part of me wanted to slam the door in her face for how she ended things between us, but I couldn't bring myself to do it.

Instead, I stepped back, permitting her to enter. Her familiar fragrance wafted past my nose when she passed me. It had been years, but the smell was the same. It used to be my favorite. She took a few steps into my living room before looking at me. Without speaking, she glided towards me and gently placed her lips against mine. I hadn't felt her lips, let alone her touch, in years, so it should've felt foreign. It didn't. It was so familiar it was scary. I started to kiss her back but stopped myself and gently pushed her away.

"I'm sorry," she blurted out, "it's just, it's been a long time. Almost like déjà vu."

"It's been a minute," I agreed.

"So, you gon' pour me a drink and tell me about your life? Are you seeing anyone? Are you *in love* now?" she asked, animated.

"You really gon stand here and shoot the shit with me like we're two old friends? You said you wanted to talk, so talk," I encouraged her, heading back into the kitchen to refill my glass and pour her one. There was no way I would make it through the conversation without a buzz.

She sighed while resting her back against the island. "You want answers, right? I know I owe you that."

I scraped my hand over my face before rolling the tension from my shoulders. "You fuckin' right you do."

Her chest hitched as she tried to speak. When nothing came out, she started fiddling with her fingers. It was the same nervous tick she'd always had. "Judah, I—I'm sorry for what happened between us all those years ago. You know I never would've just up and left like that, but there was so much going on at the time, and we were so young, y'know? I wasn't in control of all my decisions or my emotions. Plus, you know how my parents were. When they said jump, Valencia and I had to say how high? After I lost the baby, they wanted a fresh start."

My face was livid with anger. "You let them tear us apart."

"I was already so depressed after losing the baby. So, three days before the funeral, they told Valencia and me we were moving. Then, the morning after the funeral, we packed up the last of our things and moved to Texas," she reasoned.

"And yet this is the first time I hear from you in, what? Ten years? You could've called, texted, or anything. Hell, you could've written a fuckin' letter. Anything would've been better than the nothing I got," I argued before taking a swig of my drink.

"I couldn't stay in Miami after that. My family was leaving! I'd have nowhere to go."

I felt my cheeks grow warm before I shouted. "You could've come to me!"

Silent tears slipped down her cheeks. "I was trapped in a bubble of sadness back then; I barely remember putting one foot in front of the other. I had nowhere to turn."

"You were supposed to turn to me, Jas!" My voice lashed at her. "Our fuckin' son died, Jasmin. Elijah died. And you left me to pick up all the pieces by myself. Now, you stand here after all this time, and you can't even say his name! Say his name! Elijah! His name is Elijah!"

She pointed an accusatory finger. "I know his name!" she choked out before a tear slipped from the corner of her eye.

I leaned over the island, burying my head in my hands. Seconds later, I felt her warm presence near me, trying to console me. I shrugged her off before pinching my lips together. Anger and nerves shook my voice. "Y'know, I had to run down on your cousin to find out that you up and moved to Texas! I ain't change my number for years waiting for you, thinking one day you'd call, or show up, anything with some information. Anything that made more sense than how you left things," I muttered, shaking my head.

"Judah, I know, I—"

There was a painful tightening in my throat as I inched out the words. "You broke my fuckin' heart, yo. And it wasn't until today that I realized I ain't never get over that shit."

She clutched her stomach. "Listen to me. It *killed* me to leave you and walk away from everything like that! *Killed* me! But I was drowning in Miami! I was just so fucking sad. All I wanted to do was be with Elijah, and because I knew I couldn't, all I did was cry myself to sleep every night. And as the months and years rolled by, it got harder and harder for me to reach out. I didn't know what to say, and a part of me figured you wanted me to stay away, so I—I just kept telling myself that you were better off without me." Her voice faded.

I scoffed. "More like you were better off without me."

"You know how much I loved you. A part of me still does," she admitted, confession cutting like a whip across my heart.

I cut my eyes at her, jaw clenched tight. "You said all you need to say?"

"Y—yeah, that's it."

"Cool. There's the door," I snapped, failing to conceal my bitterness.

Her facial expression went from sad to surprise, and then she settled back on sad. She was trying to cope with the fact that I didn't care, even though I did. Internally, I was fighting back the urge to hold her in my arms, but my pride wouldn't let me move a muscle. She turned toward the door and placed her hand on the knob before turning around.

Her chin trembled. "I—I still celebrate his birthday, y'know? Every year," she responded in a zombie-like voice while brushing a teardrop from her cheek.

She dipped her chin so I wouldn't see her face screwed up when more tears started slipping from the corners of her eyes. A frown clouded my face as my head swam with thoughts. I was never good at reading anybody but Jasmin, and all those feelings I thought had faded all those years ago had suddenly resurfaced, and the air got thin. I told Skai it was over between us. That I felt nothing. But one look in her eyes, and I was right back to the seventeen-year-old boy head-over-heels in love with her. In some twisted way, our hearts were still tethered together. I hated how much I still loved her. I approached her, arms encircling her slender waist before I tilted her chin toward my face so that her eyes had no choice but to make contact with mine.

She buried her head in my chest. "I still miss him so much."

"Me too," I confided in her, fingers sliding down her arms and leaving their warmth on her smooth skin.

Jasmin looked up at me, staring into my glossy eyes, fluid still free falling down her cheeks. I searched her eyes for some clue as to what was going on in her mind, but I could tell her thoughts were all over the place like mine. Somehow my lips made their way to hers, pressing her wet face against mine. She circled her arms around my neck as I grabbed her waist and pulled her body closer to mine before inserting my tongue inside her mouth. She let out a soft moan and wrestled her tongue against mine. I slowly caressed her body, easing the back of her shirt up her back. My lips clung to her while picking her up and pressing her body against the back of the door. She palmed the back of my head, moaning as I kissed down her chest. She quickly pulled her shirt over her head and tossed it to the ground. My fingertips spread across her lean, freckled shoulders before sliding down to caress her breasts. I toyed with her hardened nipples before taking one into my mouth and flicking my tongue against it. She tossed her head back, moaning and twisting her legs around my waist.

"Shit, hold up," I objected, releasing her from my grasp.

"What's wrong?" she asked, panting and moaning against my lips.

"I'm supposed to be over us. The past just can't come back up like this. I'm sorry, but I can't do this shit."

"Judah, please. I let my parents force you out of my life once, and now that I'm back, I'm not gonna let you run me back out. I won't," she protested.

"I used to think about you every second of the day when you first left. Playing back everything in my head that went down between us in the days leading up to when you left. And now that you're back, and I've heard your side of the story, I don't know that it makes a difference."

"What do you mean?"

My neck sliced left and then right. I had to keep it G with her. "I still don't think I can forgive you...."

She pressed her lavender-scented skin against mine. "We've been given a second chance. I know you feel it too," she whispered against my lips before tracing the tattoo of her name on my neck.

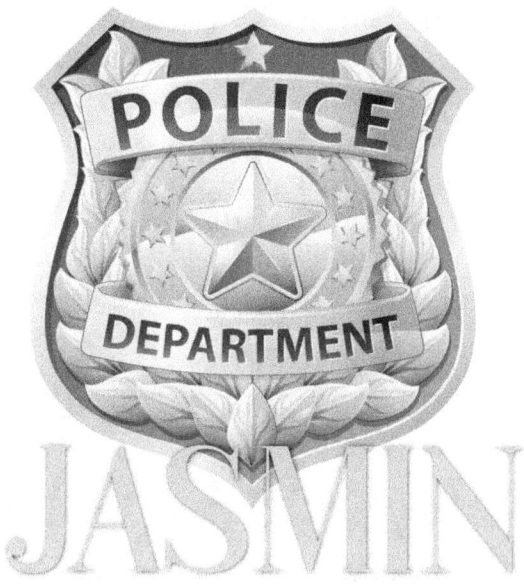

JASMIN

THE WEEKS FLEW BY, AND I COULDN'T KEEP JUDAH OFF MY MIND, NOR did I want to. My mind was tainted with thoughts of him. It was the first time I felt such a strong connection to someone again. I'd never been the type to be interested in flings or one-night stands, always valuing deeper emotional connections over mere physical ones. It was clear that Judah and I still fit like two pieces of the same puzzle. For weeks, I found myself fantasizing about how our bodies danced across the sheets for hours or how we laid naked, wrapped in nothing but each other's arms. Being in his arms again after so many years was such a beautiful feeling. I'd dated, but no relationship had ever been able to top the relationship I shared with Judah. He was one of one, and our love was something that happened only once in a lifetime. I'd been trying to respect him enough to give him his space. He made it clear that allowing me back into his life wasn't an easy decision for him to make and that he needed time to sort out his thoughts about it all.

My phone chimed, releasing me from the entrapment of my

thoughts. I looked at the screen, and my stomach began to churn. I'd been fighting waves of nausea since I woke up and decided to make some tea to settle it. My eyes darted from left to right across the screen, reading a text from Bankx, then quickly tossed it on the countertop and dashed to the bathroom to empty my guts in the toilet bowl. After brushing my teeth to rid my mouth of the sour taste, I shot out of the bathroom to call Martinez.

He answered on the fourth ring. "Hello?"

"Martinez! What are you doing right now? I need you to get me something!"

"What?"

"A pregnancy test," I mumbled, suddenly feeling the urge to hurl again.

"Are you fucking kidding me, Jasmin? You're fucking criminals now?"

"No, no. It's nothing like that! I've just been feeling a little nauseous for the past few days, and I want to rule it out!"

"You just asked me to get you a pregnancy test while you're supposed to be undercover. Are you trying to fuck everything up?"

"No, I'm not. I've got a handle on it; I swear I do. Can you please just get me what I asked for? You're the only one I trust. He can't find out I'm anywhere near a test, or it'll blow everything up. He still thinks I'm celibate, remember?"

He sucked his teeth. "Fine."

"Thank you. I'll meet you at your place in an hour."

"Well?" Martinez asked, brow raised after I walked out of his bathroom.

"It's positive," I admitted.

"Man, fuck!" he yelled, throwing up his hands. "Who the hell have you been fucking while undercover?"

"It was a random guy, just a one-night stand to blow off some steam," I lied.

I was aware of his history with Judah and his brothers. My reconnection with Judah was no one's business but ours.

He shook his head. "You're in too fuckin' deep, Baker."

"I'm too close to getting everything we need. I can't pull out now. I won't."

"That's your problem! You're trying to be the hero and didn't do anything but entangle yourself in the web even more by making reckless decisions and sleeping around with God knows who and getting pregnant! What the fuck are you gonna do?"

"Don't worry about me. I'll think of something."

"It's not you that I'm worried about. It's this operation. What did I tell you from the beginning? Don't fuck this—"

"*Yeah, yeah.* Don't fuck this up for you. I got it," I replied, eyes rolling skyward.

"Do you?"

I sighed. "Yeah, I do."

"I don't think you know how much danger you've put yourself in. Do you know what he'll do to you if he finds out?"

"Damnit, Martinez, I didn't share this with you for you to throw it back in my face!" I griped. "I said I'll figure it out, and I will."

"You better hope so, for everybody's sake."

He was right; I had to be careful with Bankx. He couldn't find out I was pregnant because he'd know it wasn't his and that I was lying about being celibate. I had to ensure we took him and his uncle down sooner than later.

"Hey, I, um, I know why you wanna take down Bankx and his uncle, but what's your obsession with the Snow family?" I quizzed.

"You mean other than the fact that they're scum?"

"Yeah, besides that."

"Where'd that question come from?"

"I saw some of the files on your desk. I know you've been chasing them for a while now. C'mon, humor me," I encouraged him.

He shrugged. "People like them don't deserve to walk freely amongst the rest of us."

"Exactly what kind of people are they?"

"Fuckin' animals," he growled, "but enough about them. I wanna know what your plan is."

He'd said enough for me to know there was more to the story. I promised myself I would investigate it the first chance I got, but I needed to get in touch with Judah to tell him that we were expecting another baby together.

"I'll tell you when I find out myself."

BABY

SINCE WE SMASHED, I'D BEEN DODGING JASMIN'S CALLS AND TEXTS FOR weeks. I promised myself that it was a one-time thing and wouldn't happen again, especially since Skai and I had made up, and things between us were good. I wanted to put all my attention into building our relationship and finally put a period at the end of a decade-long sentence. The more time I spent with Skai, the guiltier I felt about fucking around with Jasmin. As much as I wanted there to be nothing between us, my denial was no match for the history we shared. Nevertheless, I pushed her to the back of my mind, determined never to look in my rearview again.

My phone began to vibrate, stirring me out of my thoughts. I glanced at the screen to see a number I didn't recognize, but it had a Miami area code.

"The fuck is this?" I answered.

"It's me. Please don't hang up," Jasmin sputtered.

I scoffed. "You callin' me from different numbers now?"

"It's the only way I could get you to talk to me. I've been the one reaching out. You're the one who ghosted me," she confirmed.

K.L. Hall

"Look, I ain't got time to talk to you right now. What do you want?"

"What do I want? So, it's like that now? I thought we had an understanding."

"And what kind of understanding was that? You show up here after all these years sayin' you want closure, I give you that, and more, and now you still on my line. What the fuck is up with you, Jasmin? For real?" I griped, seconds away from hanging up.

"I wanted to tell you this in person, but it doesn't look like you'll allow me to do that."

"Tell me what?"

"I'm pregnant, Judah."

"What the fuck that got to do with me?" I grumbled.

"It's yours."

My eyebrows strained for my hairline. "Stop fuckin' with me, Jas."

"I wish I were, but I'm not. I'm telling the truth," she insisted, "and you would've known sooner if you'd returned any of the numerous calls and texts I sent you."

I knew how sex worked, and I knew better than to play the 'but I only hit it one-time' card with her. Instead, I fell silent for a few seconds to collect at least one of my thoughts. "How far along are you?"

She sighed. "Four and a half weeks."

"You been to the doctor already?"

"Yes. I had an appointment yesterday to confirm. I go back at eight weeks for my ultrasound. Look, I know this was a lot for me to dump on you, and again, not how I wanted you to find out, but I think we should look at this as something positive.

"And why is that?"

"This could be our second chance. I know we can't turn back the clock and bring Elijah back, but now we can be the family we both always wanted."

"That's the thing, Jas. We're not those seventeen, eighteen-year-olds we were when you left the first time. I'm invested in other shit now."

"You mean you're invested in other people now."

I kissed my teeth. "Whatever."

"Listen, I'm not asking you to propose to me or for us to move in together. You have time to tell whoever you need to tell. Just don't wait forever."

"So, that's it? You're keeping it?"

"Are you really standing in my face asking me that right now? Of course, I am."

"Wow, Jas."

"Wow? You can think what you want, but I didn't come back here to blow up your life, Judah."

"Yeah, well, it sure fuckin' feels that way!"

"How many times do I have to say that I know what happened all those years ago hurt you? They hurt me too! I'm sorry for the part I played in it, but I was seventeen! I had no real choice back then, which is why I keep telling you that I think we've been given a second chance now. I want this baby, Judah. I want another chance to have *your* baby," she confirmed.

I parted my lips to speak, but nothing came out. Instead, I pulled the phone away from my ear to see that Skai was beeping in. A long sigh etched out my nostrils. "Look, I gotta go."

"Oh—okay."

I clicked over to answer for Skai. "Hey."

"Hey, you. What's up? What are you doing?"

"Nothing. What's up?"

"Well, I've got some good news."

"And what's that?"

"It looks like I'll be having an early night. I should be home around six. I thought maybe we could pick up dinner at my favorite Thai spot, find something to binge on Netflix, and see where the night takes us. What do you think?" she proposed.

"Ah, um, yeah. That, uh, that sounds good," I responded, halfway listening.

I couldn't get Jasmin's words out of my head. Her pregnancy meant there was no way I could continue hiding what happened between us from Skai. She deserved to know the truth sooner than later, and I wanted to make sure she heard it from me. But could I break her heart? No matter what I felt, I knew the answer had to be yes. I opened my mouth to speak, but I couldn't bring myself to say the words.

"Hello? Ju? Are you there?"

My neck sliced left and right. "Huh? Y–yeah. I'm here. Sorry."

"So, I'll see you tonight?"

"Yeah," I confirmed. "See you tonight."

SKAI

JU WAS IN MY HEAD, EVEN WHEN HE WASN'T SUPPOSED TO BE. HE WAS the invader of my waking and subconscious thoughts. Anytime he crossed my mind, I felt a flutter in my chest. Anytime I saw him, I lit up like a kid at Christmas. I was comfortable in his presence. For weeks, my mind had been fighting what my heart already knew. I was in love, and I couldn't hold it in anymore. I had to tell him.

After work, I swung by my favorite Thai spot to pick up dinner and got back to my place just in time to take a shower and set the mood. He showed up at my apartment at seven o'clock, smelling like he'd just finished smoking three or four blunts and with an apprehensive look on his face.

"Hey!"

He pulled me into a warm hug. "Hey."

"I've been excited to see you all day," I informed him before placing small kisses on the corner of his mouth then pressing my lips against his.

"Word?"

I looked up at him, smiling for no reason. "Yeah."

"It smells good in here."

"Yup. I picked up some Thai for dinner like I told you I would."

"Oh, yeah."

"Are you okay?"

He nodded. "Y–yeah. I'm fine."

"Do you wanna eat now or head over to the couch and figure out what we're gonna watch?" I inquired.

"The couch is cool," he grumbled, marching ahead of me.

I eyed him from across the room, my stomach filled with anxious butterflies as I made my way over to join him on the couch. I'd planned to tell him we needed to "talk" after dinner and a few episodes but holding it in became like holding my breath underwater. My heart may as well have been a hammer beating in my chest. Excitement coursed through my entire body. My heart was so full of love I thought I would explode. The longer I waited, the harder it became to hold it in.

"I have something I need to talk to you about, er, tell you," the words jolted nervously from my throat.

"I gotta talk to you about something, too," he replied with a sigh.

"Oh, okay, um, do you mind if I go first? I've been kind of like replaying this in my head over and over all day, and I just wanna finally get it off my chest."

"Okay."

"I mean, it's not like a long speech or anything. It's more like a feeling, y'know? And I wanna be upfront with you about my feelings…about you…a–and me. You and me." I nervously ran my fingers through my hair. "I guess what I'm trying to say is, I enjoy spending time with you, and you've become someone very special to me. I can't even believe I'm about to say this, but I–I'm falling in love with y–"

He held out his hand to stop me. "Skai, stop."

"What?"

"Please don't say what I think you're about to say."

"W–what do you mean? Why not?"

"I don't want you to tell me you're in love with me because I don't want you to love me, Skai. I don't deserve it."

"Of course you do. Why would you say that?" I asked, cupping his cheeks in my small hands.

He quickly pulled my hands away. "Because I don't."

"I know you're scarred from your past, but that's just the thing, it's the past, and if that's over like you said, then I need to know what's so wrong with me falling in love with you. Because this is the happiest I've been in a long time, Ju, and I mean that," I gushed, heart swelling with emotion.

He shot up from the couch. "Stop it, Skai! Just fuckin' stop it, please. Aight? You're making everything ten times harder."

My brows scrunched in confusion. "Ju, tell me what's going on with you. You've been off since you got here."

"I fucked Jasmin," he confessed, eyes grazing the floor.

My heart shook at the words. "W–what?"

He drew his guilt-ridden eyes up to mine. "And she's pregnant, Skai. It's mine."

My heart sank to the floor. I was vexed, green-eyed, and broken all at the same time. All this time, I thought he was too broken to love me back when in reality, his heart still belonged to another woman.

"Correct me if I've been reading this all wrong, but I thought you and me, we were–I–I thought. No. Th–this doesn't make any sense. I gave you a real chance, and y–you. We had a good thing, Ju. You know we did. Nah, you fucked this up to protect yourself. You were just looking for a reason to mess this up!" I accused.

"Skai–"

"No!"

"I'm sorry. I–I never wanted shit to go down this way."

"How long has this been going on behind my back?"

"It happened after we had that big blowout, and it was only one time."

"So, you've been lying to me for weeks?"

He shook his head. "I fucked up, but I didn't lie to you. I just found out today!"

"You lied when you didn't tell me after it happened. You lied, and you lied, and you lied, and like the fucking idiot I am, I believed you! I believed you when you said it was over and all that shit with her was in the past. I mean, the fact that you still have her fucking name tattooed on the side of your neck should've been enough for me! If that's not testament enough to not being over your ex, then I don't know what is."

"I don't know what else to say other than I'm sorry."

"And what exactly are you sorry for, huh? Fucking your ex behind my back or getting caught up in the same web she strung you in when you were teenagers!"

"Skai–"

"No! Here's a hard truth for you, Judah. You two went through a terrible, unimaginable thing all those years ago, and she *left* your ass! She left you all alone to pick up the pieces! And you let her come back to Miami and into your life for what? Closure? The disrespect you got when she left all those years ago was all the closure you needed, but you still went back for more! And if you play stupid games, guess what you gon' win? Stupid fuckin' prizes."

"Fuck you, Skai!" he thundered.

"Fuck me? Fuck you!"

"You about to cross a line you shouldn't," he warned.

"Why should any of that matter now? I'm done."

"Don't say that."

"Don't say what? Are you kidding me right now? What is left for me here? You're having a baby with the only woman you've ever loved. She wins!"

He reached out for me, and I pulled away. "Do you know how bad I wanna tell you I love you back? But I know better than to say it when I can't give you what you need right now."

"You can't love me. You wouldn't do what you did if you only loved me. And even if what you say is true, and you do love me, you still love her, too, and I can't compete with that. I won't. I hope you fall and break your heart over her just like I did for you. Now get the fuck out of my apartment," I demanded, tears rolling down my cheeks.

"Skai—please."

My teeth clenched angrily around the words. "Get the fuck out!" I screamed, heart breaking.

SKAI

ONE WEEK LATER.

Ever since the night I kicked Ju out of my apartment, I felt like I was on a runaway train going one hundred miles per hour with no signs of stopping. I could barely stomach the fact that he'd cheated on me, let alone the news about her pregnancy. In my eyes, he was Malik 2.0. I was done wasting my time with men who were unavailable, both physically and emotionally. I deserved to have someone love me out loud, and if Ju wanted to waste time and energy chasing after the woman who'd already broken his heart once, then I wasn't going to stick around and wait for him to come to his senses when she did it again. His confession only solidified what I already knew to be true; he picked a side the day he chased her down outside the restaurant on *our* date. As furious as I was and as played as I felt, I'd never felt a Miami night so cold without him.

To stop my mind from spiraling out of control any longer, I picked up my phone and started strolling through my social media timelines. I'd been so wrapped up in Ju and my career that I realized I hadn't posted a picture since the night Jade and I went to that bachelor party. I sighed before going to my camera roll to replay the videos we'd made and the pictures we'd taken that night. My teary-eyed walk down memory lane with pictures of us somehow turned into photos of Ju and me. A huff pushed past my lips while I debated whether to send a text, call, or none of the above.

"No, Skai! No! Fuck him! He made his choice!" I yelled from the confinement of my queen bed.

I had to face the fact that there wasn't room enough in his heart for the both of us. I must have picked up my phone and put it down a million times in the last hour alone, so I decided to call the one person who I knew would always keep it real with me. The phone didn't even bother to connect before I heard Jade's voice on the other end of the phone.

"It's your girl, Jade. I can't make it to the phone because a bitch is out here livin' life! Leave a message, and maybe I'll call you back."

"God, I miss you." I sighed into the receiver as soon as her voicemail beeped. The line fell silent for a few seconds before I started up again. "Like, why do boys have to be so fuckin' stupid, huh? All they do is take and take. Fuckin' siphoning all a bitch love, all a bitch heart, and for what? He went and had a baby on me, Jade! And I was gonna tell him I loved him. How stupid am I?" I scoffed before hanging up.

Hearing myself say those words outside my head sounded foreign, so I was glad no one else was around to listen to them. I closed my eyes, hearing her voice as clear as day inside my head. If she had been listening on the other line, she would've said, *"See, that's what your ass gets for wasting your time with boys instead of grown-ass men. Don't let nobody pick and choose when they wanna fuck with you. It's gotta be all the way or no way. You too grown and too damn pretty for inconsistency and fuck nigga shit!"*

Then in my defense, I would rebuttal with a question, asking her what was so wrong with wanting to be loved correctly, and she'd say something like, *"See, that's your problem. You wanna be wifed so bad when dating out here with these niggas is like putting all your trust in a public defender, okay?"*

Then we'd laugh, and she'd continue to make jokes about my love life and how I was too tender for the streets to try and lift my spirits. I didn't know if I was capable of completely turning off my feelings for Ju or how long it would take for my bruised heart and ego to heal, but in the meantime, I was going to focus on work and put my career first. I couldn't force Ju to choose me. If he felt he could do better with Jasmin because of the past they shared, what else could I do but let him? But he may as well have sold his ears because he would never hear from me again.

Four weeks later.

A month passed, and I was mentally done mourning my relationship with Ju. Yet, emotionally, I'd only allowed myself to dust the cobwebs off my Bumble and Tinder profiles to reactivate them just to have someone to talk to outside of work. After chatting here and there with random beaus, the time and opportunity aligned for me to go out on an actual date. As scarred as my heart still was, and as much as I dreaded the idea of starting over and finding out all the likes and dislikes of someone new, I didn't have any other choice. It was either mix and mingle or continue to let my feelings hold me hostage inside my apartment.

There I was, all dolled up, at the candlelit cocktail table at a rooftop bar awaiting my date, Peter. I took one more scroll through his dating profile. He'd been a CPA for four years, drove a silver Mercedes C-Class coupe, and was into HGTV and anime just as much as I was. We seemed like a good fit on paper, but only time would be the judge of that. Perhaps the only thing I could prejudge him about was that he was white. Being biracial, I didn't have a problem dating either side of my race, but I would always make white men work harder. Maybe it was because my father was white, and I saw the amount of privilege that came with that, so I felt the need to make white men jump through higher hoops to be with me.

Nevertheless, he wouldn't have been the first medium-rare dick I'd sat on over the years. They never lasted long, but maybe good old Pete would be different. He'd managed to make it through the first few hoops, which was promising. I made sure to get his political opinions and worldviews on the table early. The last fucking thing I wanted to do was to let a Trump supporter sweep me off my feet.

"Skai?"

I twisted my neck to see an average-height white man wearing a navy blazer over a crisp white tee and cargo pants bobbing towards me with a pep in his step. I wasn't sure if that was my first red flag or not, but I allowed him to approach me anyway.

"Peter?"

"That's me," he answered before taking his seat next to me at the bar. "I must admit, you're more beautiful than your pictures."

My brows puckered. "Isn't that what everyone says the first time they see someone in real life who they first met online? It like never fails."

He chuckled. "Yeah. You're probably right about that being a cliche line, but in this case, it's the truth."

I grinned. "Well, thank you."

I gave him a once-over up close. He, too, looked better in person, even with his Jonas Brother haircut. He had a crop of dark auburn hair and a tanned face that accentuated his brilliant blue eyes. Although his chin looked as if it hadn't seen a razor in over a week, his fingernails were bright and white with no dirt in sight.

"Shall we get our date started?"

"We shall."

An hour passed, and all I'd managed to retain about him was that he was kinda tall, cute, and a fucking snooze fest. He spent so much time reiterating the same shit we'd talked about through text or FaceTime, like what he did in his spare time, what anime he was currently binging, and where he grew up.

"So, what wine are we having?" he asked before my phone began to vibrate against the white polyester tablecloth.

I quickly flipped it over to look at the screen. "I'm sorry, it's the hospital. I've got to take this," I informed him before excusing myself from the table.

I'd never been so happy to see the hospital calling in my life. The lord must have heard my silent prayer to fast forward through the night. After returning to the table, I gave Peter my apologies and told him that our emergency room was backed up and I had to go in.

"I'll uh; I'll text you," I told him with a forced smile.

"Yeah, sure thing. Go save lives!"

"I'll try."

Clad in my periwinkle blue scrubs, my ears tuned into the symphony of wailing, murmuring, and coughing amongst patients in the waiting room. The ER was filled with a myriad of patients with varying degrees of illness and injury. I could smell the blood in the air and knew it would be one of those nights.

"Incoming!" Lawrence, the chief resident, yelled.

I made my way around the E.R. nurses' station, and the automatic doors whooshed as I ran out to meet the stretcher coming off the back of the ambulance.

"Female, twenty-seven, collapsed inside a retail store. She just started to come to inside the ambulance and has been complaining of severe pain in her abdomen," the female paramedic informed me.

"Did she give you any information?" I asked, sliding my pen inside my scrub pocket.

"I'm seven and a half weeks pregnant," the patient muttered, pulling the oxygen mask away from her face.

I slid my pen inside my scrub pocket before peering down at her. "Hi, I'm Dr. Daniels. Can you tell–"

Instantly, I froze when I realized the woman on the stretcher was Ju's ex, Jasmin. She stared back at me with anxiety and worry written across her face, not sharing my same surprise in recognizing who I was before passing out again. I quickly cleared my throat, trying to regain my composure, and pull my lip up off the floor. Back inside the hospital, I pulled the dividing curtain to separate her from the other E.R. patients. I immediately noticed her abdomen was tender and rigid on the left side, and she had heavy vaginal bleeding.

"Page Dr. Thomas in OB and let her know we're on our way up," I told the nurse.

An ultrasound by the OB attending proved what I had already presumed to be true; Jasmin was suffering from an ectopic pregnancy, and her fallopian tube had ruptured. To avoid any more blood loss, Dr. Thomas decided to book an operating room for emergency surgery.

"Daniels, get ready to scrub in."

"M–me?" I questioned.

"Yes. I'll see you in the OR."

I stepped into the OR, inhaling the sterile, bleach-like smell. Life was so fucking surreal, I could barely stand it. The woman carrying the child of the man I loved was lying on the operating table in front of me, and I was assisting Dr. Thomas in her surgery.

"Is she going to be okay?" I asked Dr. Thomas after the surgery was complete.

"She's lost a lot of blood, but yes. She's going to be okay. I just hope she wasn't too attached to the pregnancy."

"Right..."

"Good call on this case, Daniels. It was your quick thinking that saved this woman's life. Page me when she wakes up."

I bobbed my head. "Thank you, Dr. Thomas. Will do."

My entire time inside the OR, I felt invigorated, untouchable even. There was no time or space to feel anything or do anything other than the work I'd been trained to do. That peerless, exceptional feeling evaporated when I stepped out of the OR, and I broke down immediately in the privacy of the nearest bathroom stall. My shoulder shook uncontrollably as my adrenaline boost plummeted to the ground. That was it. Ju's baby was gone. I'd spent so many nights hating them both to exhaustion, only for her to lose *another* baby and a fallopian tube. I hated myself even more for how relieved I felt about it all.

Hours after her surgery, I walked into her private recovery room to examine her. I drew the blinds, standing silently at her door with an uneasy feeling coursing through my stomach. My eyes pinged from one pale wall to the next, the whiteboard with her information on it, the metal IV with saline bag, and the chart at the foot of her bed.

Feelings aside, I slowly approached her, attempting not to wake her as I pulled a set of small/medium gloves from the box on the wall and snapped them over my cold, sterilized hands. Awakening from the anesthesia, she flinched at the cold shock of my stethoscope against her skin. She sluggishly twisted her neck in my direction as the intense fluorescent lights above her caused her to squint.

"What happened?"

"Hi. I'm Dr. Daniels. How are you feeling?"

"Groggy and confused."

"Do you remember anything about how you got here?"

"I remember being in the checkout line in the store when I started having these excruciating cramps on my left side. Then all of a sudden, I started to get lightheaded. Next thing I know, I'm waking up in the back of an ambulance, and then it's all spotty from there. Can you fill me in?"

"Um, Dr. Thomas will be in to check on you in a little bit, and she can answer any questions you may have," I confirmed.

She licked her chapped lips, still groggy from the pain medication. "It's bad, isn't it?"

"Let me go get Dr. Thomas for you."

"You're a doctor, too, right?"

"Yes."

"Then just tell me now."

I sighed. "When you came in, you were losing a lot of blood, and we discovered that your left fallopian tube had ruptured. Dr. Thomas had to perform surgery to remove it."

"And the baby?"

I lowered my gaze to her chart at the foot of the bed. "I'm sorry, but there was nothing we could do."

The lifeless room fell silent as she twisted her lips to fight her tears. "Take a minute to yourself. I'm going to go check on your labs and see if I can snag Dr. Thomas for you."

Ten minutes later, I returned to Jasmin's room with Dr. Thomas in tow. I took my place by the door, zoning out to the beeping of her heart monitor while Dr. Thomas approached her bedside.

"Hi, Jasmin. I'm Dr. Thomas, the OB that operated on you. Dr. Daniels informed me that you had some questions."

"I just want to know what happened."

Dr. Thomas pushed her fingers through her golden curls before speaking. "I'm sorry to inform you of this, Ms. Baker, but you suffered from an ectopic pregnancy. When you came in, you'd already lost a lot of blood, and we had to perform an emergency laparoscopic surgery to save you. Unfortunately, there was too much damage, and we couldn't save the fetus or your left fallopian tube."

Her lip trembled. "W–what?"

"I understand this may be a challenging time for you, Ms. Baker, but the good news is that you're going to be okay. You'll be in pain for a bit, but if all continues to go well, you'll be discharged in a few days."

"A *few days?*"

"Yes. Dr. Daniels and I will continue monitoring your HCG levels to ensure they continue to go down and that the pregnancy was removed properly."

"How soon can I try and get pregnant again if that's what I want?" she inquired, a silent tear trickling down the side of her nose.

Dr. Thomas sighed before propping herself up at the foot of Jasmin's hospital bed. "Right now, your body needs time to heal. And if conceiving another child is something you want to do in the future, I'm not saying it's impossible, but be prepared to have a long road ahead of you," she advised.

"Is there anyone we can notify?" Dr. Thomas quizzed with a comforting touch on her shoulder.

"No," she answered quickly.

"Not even the father?" I blurted out, face pale at the thought.

"No."

"Having someone to escort you is the only way we'll be able to discharge you," I informed her.

Dr. Thomas snapped her neck in my direction as if to tell me to shut up. "But for now, get some rest."

She patted her leg before exiting the room, looking for me to follow her out. I turned my neck to face Jasmin once more.

"Are you sure there's no one you want me to call? You really shouldn't be alone at a time like this."

"I said no! I don't want to call anyone. I'm fine. Just close the door on your way out," she demanded, ice in her voice.

Three days passed, and Dr. Thomas was ready to discharge Jasmin from her care. Until then, I made sure I limited our interaction, only dropping in to do exams and lab work when necessary. I was glad I didn't have to bear witness to her life, especially when she had no idea how closely it interfered with mine. I knocked on her hospital room door, ready to deliver the good news, and paused to see no one in the bed.

"Jasmin? W–where are y–?" I heard the toilet flush before finishing the rest of my sentence.

She slowly made her way out of the bathroom. "Hey…"

"Hey. I'm, um, just here to drop off your discharge papers. Do you have someone to take you home?"

"Yeah. My uh, boyfriend is downstairs."

Her words pinched my chest. I wasn't ready to face Ju. I didn't want to witness him in another moment of grief when a part of me was still grieving over him. But at the end of the day, my duty trumped my feelings. Before I could find the words to respond, Dr. Thomas walked in. "Ah, I see Dr. Daniels made it with your discharge papers."

"Yup."

I exhaled. "Uh, yeah. Here you go," I said, handing her the clipboard.

"Do you have someone to escort you home?" she repeated my question.

"Yeah. My boyfriend is downstairs," she repeated.

"Good. Once you've signed, Dr. Daniels will escort you to the doors to ensure you get to your ride alright."

"Do you need to? You know what, it's fine. Never mind," she griped, scribbling her name on the line across the dotted lines.

"Take care of yourself."

"Yeah, thanks."

"Wheelchair or walk?" I asked once the two of us were alone again.

"I can walk," she answered, ripping the I.D. band off her wrist and tossing it in the trash.

"Alright, let's go."

The entire elevator ride was so silent you would've been able to hear a pin drop if it hadn't been for the dinging between each floor. My heart was racing with dread and nerves. I hadn't laid eyes on him since he told me the news of her pregnancy. I knew I would probably be the last person he wanted to see. The automatic doors whooshed open, and she started making her way over to a big-body truck with the engine grumbling.

"That's my ride. I got it from here," she informed me.

I frowned, not recognizing that he'd gotten a new ride. The driver hopped out, and I froze to see Bankx stalking toward us with a grimace on his face. "Yo, I can't get a call from you tellin' me to pick you up with no explanation, baby."

"I'm fine, bae. It's nothing," she told him, cupping his face in her hands.

He glanced down at her while pulling her hands away from him. "Nah. What the hell happened? This where you been for the past few days?"

"Yeah, but I'm fine, right?" she asked, glancing back at me.

He glared at me, searching my eyes for the truth. I bobbed silently. "She's okay."

"What the fuck happened to you?"

"Appendicitis," she answered, eyes dead set on mine, "I had my appendix removed."

My antennas went up as I swiveled on my heels, ready to disappear into the depths of the hospital. My mind was exploding with questions. As unprepared as I was to stand face-to-face with Ju again, Bankx was the last person I expected to see. Where did that leave Ju? Was she dating them both? Whose baby did she lose, and which one of them would she come clean to? I may have helped to save her life, but I knew from the moment I laid eyes on Jasmin that she wasn't shit. She was a manipulative snake, catching nigga after nigga in her inescapable web of lies and bullshit.

SKAI

FIVE DAYS LATER.

As much as I wanted to keep Ju and all his drama in a land far, far away from me, I seemed to keep running into it unexpectedly. I couldn't believe I had to witness Jasmin losing their unborn child *and* find out she had been cheating on him with the man who murdered my best friend. I still got chills whenever Bankx's face popped into my head. He was indeed a walking nightmare. I remained lost in thought while going through the motions of my day. After my shift ended, I tossed my crossbody bag over my shoulder and headed toward the elevator. The big metal box only managed to move down one floor before coming to a temporary halt. With my eyes cast downward, I let out a wide-mouthed yawn just before the door opened completely.

"What up, Skai?"

My head shot up at the familiar yet unwelcomed greeting, and I immediately cursed myself for choosing the elevator over the stairs. "Hey…"

"It's been a lil' minute. Haven't seen you around in a while," Malik stated.

"I guess it has." I frowned then shrugged my shoulders, unwilling to reflect on our past.

"You been good?"

I cut my eyes at him. "We don't have to do this, y'know?"

"Do what?"

"Have awkward small talk at work after seeing each other naked as often as we have. We're adults. What happened between us is done and over with. You don't owe me shit."

His thick, bushy eyebrows rose in surprise. "Damn, so it's like that?"

"What other way is there for it to be?"

"True. Well, I'll officially be off the market by the end of the week."

I dipped my chin in a curt nod, knowing he wasn't the type to *stay* off the market regardless of what a piece of paper said. "Congrats."

The elevator dinged before he could edge out his following sentence, and I skated through the sliver without looking back. I'd finally learned how to stop fueling that fire, and I felt more liberated than I had in a long time because of it. It was the first time I'd ever been glad to be around someone I once cared about and feel nothing. Once inside my car, I placed an order at my favorite Thai restaurant and headed across the city to pick it up before heading home. I was looking forward to a relaxing, solo Netflix & Chill night with my crab fried rice and a bottle of white wine.

With my dinner in tow, I headed out of the restaurant and back to my car when I heard another familiar voice call out to me from behind. I twisted my neck to see Ju, and my knees instantly turned to water as he made his way over to me.

"Skai, hey," he greeted me with a smile curved up the right side of his face. "I thought that was you."

I shifted my weight from one leg to the other, trying to get the feeling back in them. "Yup, it's me in the flesh."

"What you doin' out here?"

I held up my bagged meal. "Dinner. You know this is my favorite Thai spot."

"I ain't gon' lie; I've slid through here a few times for some of those bomb-ass spring rolls they got," he admitted with a soft chuckle.

"You're welcome," I replied as an unexpected smile graced my face.

It was the last facial expression I thought I'd give him if we ever ran into each other again. But there I was, cheesing while looking into his beautiful brown eyes like he hadn't trampled all over my heart.

"You look good. How you been?" he inquired.

"Um, fine. You?"

He ran his hand across the nape of his neck. "Been better, but you know that's how life goes," he said in a drawn out voice that made me feel sorry for him.

"Yeah, um, I'm sorry for your loss," I explained, briefly casting my eyes down to the pavement. The words leapt out of my mouth almost of their own accord. As soon as they did, I regretted them, instantly wishing I could take them back. Panicked, my head shot up to see him glaring down at me with a confused look on his face. A dash of wild color entered my cheeks as my pulse escalated.

"What?"

"N–nothing. Never mind. I gotta go, okay?"

"Hold up. What did you mean?"

My head shook vigorously from left to right. "It's nothing, Ju. Forget I mentioned it."

I hit my key fob to unlock my car and hurried to the driver's side door. He quickly cornered me between the door's opening; his brow puckered as he glared at me. "That's bullshit, Skai. Tell me what the hell you meant."

All I could hear was the Hippocratic Oath replaying over and over inside my head. "I'm sorry, but I can't. It'll be a HIPPA violation. Just talk to her."

He slowly released his breath. "Talk to who?"

Caught between a rock and a hard place, my nostrils exhaled a long sigh. "Wait, you really don't know what I'm talking about?"

"Not a clue, and you still ain't told me shit."

I could hear the frustration in his tone as my breath caught slightly in my throat. "Oh my God. Jasmin—she didn't tell you?" I mumbled through my fingers.

"What does she have to do with anything? What the fuck aren't you telling me, Skai?"

"Ju, I'm so sorry."

His face crinkled in annoyance. "Sorry for what, Skai? Tell me what the fuck is goin' on. What didn't Jasmin tell me?"

"I shouldn't be telling you this. I could lose my license."

"Tell me what you know, Skai," he demanded.

"S—she came into the hospital almost a week ago."

"The hospital? For what?"

"S—she lost the baby, Ju…."

His lips formed an oval of surprise. "W—what?"

"I'm so sorry! I—I only brought it up because I thought you knew!"

He stood, silently staring at me with a blank look on his face. "Nah."

"And that's not all…."

"What else is there? What else don't I know, Skai?" he quizzed, tone impassioned.

"Bankx picked her up from the hospital. He said she's his girl."

BABY

I MUST'VE CALLED JASMIN OVER A HUNDRED TIMES WHILE SPEEDING TO her apartment. I wanted, no, I needed answers, but her phone went to voicemail each time. My eyes stung with rage. It was one thing to lose our child, but to lie to me about it and to be consorting with my fuckin' enemy behind my back? It was a pain in my chest I didn't think I could feel again. I slammed the car into park, popped the trunk, and placed my gun inside the back of my jeans, ready and willing to put it to her temple to get the truth if it came down to it.

"Open the fuckin' door if you're in there, Jas. I swear to God!" I yelled from the other side of the thick door.

Fists balled tightly, I continued to bang, ready and willing to break the entire door into fragments if it came down to it. After ten minutes of consistent banging and yelling, security made their way up to her floor and demanded that I leave. They didn't know who they were fucking with and had either of their bald asses laid a hand on me, they would've found out. Instead of continuing to show my ass, I walked

180

away. They made sure to escort me down to the entrance. I stepped off, leaving her building enraged. Everything Skai told me had to be accurate, which made me wonder if the baby she lost had ever been mine in the first place.

"Man, fuck!" I yelled at the sky before placing the phone up to my ear, waiting for Rome to pick up.

"Yo?" he answered.

"You alone? We gotta talk."

"Yeah. What's up?"

I sighed into the receiver, knowing I was going into a conversation I wasn't excited to have. But I had to come clean to him about Jasmin losing our baby and what I'd learned about her ties to Bankx.

"There's something I need to tell you. And before I start, you gotta promise me you ain't gon' be on no holier than thou shit, aight? A nigga hurt right now, and I need my fuckin' brother," I confided.

"Ya tu sabes; I got you. Wassup?"

"You remember Jasmin, right?"

"Your ex, Jasmin?"

I nodded. "Yeah. Her."

"What about her? Didn't she move away like ten years ago?"

"Yeah, well, she's back."

"And?"

"And I fucked around with her again. It wasn't supposed to turn into anything serious, but shit happened, and now she's pregnant."

"Oh shit. Um, congratulations, man."

"Nah. It's far from it."

"Why? What happened?"

"She lost the baby and ain't even bother to fuckin' tell me about it."

"What the fuck? I know y'all went through a lot back in the day, but ten years is a long time. Are you sure it was yours?"

I wagged my head. "I'm not sure of anything right now."

"Wait. How'd you find out she lost the baby if she didn't tell you?"

"Skai. I ran into her earlier, and she mentioned it because she thought I already knew. You know she works at the hospital and shit."

"Yeah. Damn, yo."

"You gon' talk to her about it?"

"I've been tryin'. I'm sitting outside her apartment building, ready to put a bullet in her ass, but she ain't here."

"I know she lied to you, nigga, but a bullet? It sounds like to me you dodged one."

"You say that now, but wait until I finish tellin' you about how grimy this bitch is."

"What else she do?"

"The bitch has been fuckin' with that nigga Bankx this entire fucking time!" I stormed, getting mad all over again.

"Are you fuckin' serious, Baby? Don't play with me about no shit like that."

"I wouldn't lie to you about this," I assured him.

The line fell silent for a few seconds before Rome's emotions exploded from his mouth. "Goddamn! This mothafucka is still gunnin' for our asses on all sides! Shit! Man, fuck!"

I shook my head in a swift arc. Had I not lived it, I would've thought it was bullshit too. Our webs were more intertwined than I ever imagined, and I couldn't picture a way out that didn't involve bloodshed.

"I know. Can you just keep this shit between us? I'm not in the mood to hear that nigga Chief talk to me like I'm twelve and tell me how much of a fuck up I am."

"Don't worry about Chief. I'll handle him, aight?" Rome assured me.

"Yeah."

"And for what it's worth, I'm sorry about the baby."

"Thanks. Shit, all this time, I thought she was down for a nigga, but I swear I will *never* make the mistake of trusting her ass again," I promised.

"Hey, we all gotta learn the hard way sometimes. You've learned your lesson, right?"

"Yeah. That bitch is dead to me. I'm ready to put that mothafucka Bankx in the grave."

BABY

I SAT OUTSIDE JASMIN'S APARTMENT BUILDING FOR THREE HOURS, prepared to stake out all night if I had to, when I saw a large black truck pull up in front of her building and pull off a couple of minutes later. Jasmin stood on the curb, watching the truck drive off before turning to go inside her building. I hurried out of the car and ran up to her.

"Yo, Jas!" I shouted.

She turned her body toward the sound of my voice, one brow winged up. "Judah—w—what are you doing here?"

"When the fuck were you gonna tell me?" I raged.

Her brow creased. "Tell you what?"

"Damn, let's see. Maybe about the baby you lost or how you been fuckin' my enemy behind my back."

"W—what are you talking about?"

"Stop fuckin' lying to my face, Jasmin! I know everything."

"Okay, I just need you to calm down. Let's just go inside and talk."

"I don't wanna fuckin' talk inside. I wanna talk right here, right now!"

183

"Judah, please. Let's not cause a scene and have security come out here, okay?" She was trying her best to keep her voice even and calm, but I wasn't with the shits.

"Tell me why the fuck you didn't tell me you lost the baby!" I demanded.

"Come inside, and I swear to God, I'll tell you everything."

Jaw pinched, I trekked inside the building, following her to her apartment. Once inside, she closed the door behind her and looked at me.

"Are you calm?"

"I will be once you tell me what I came here to find out."

"Wait here, and don't move," she instructed.

I watched her run around her apartment, unplugging things before beckoning me to follow her down the hall and into the bathroom. Neither of us spoke until she turned on the shower.

"What the fuck is going on, Jasmin? I came here for the fucking truth. Now you in here actin' all secretive and shit."

"You're right; I am. But before I tell you, I need to know that I'm talking to an adult, though, Judah. Not some child."

"I'm a fuckin' grown-ass man, Jasmin. I ain't with all these lil' mind games you've been playin' with me since you fuckin' got back here! I don't even know why the fuck you even came back!"

"Things are more complicated than you realize, okay?"

"Are they? Or are you just being messy and making them that way?"

"Don't turn all this around on me when you're the one standing here yelling at me and accusing me of shit, thinking you know everything, but you don't know shit!" she yelled.

"Then, tell me why the fuck you didn't tell me you lost the baby, and I'll go! I'm out! Because from where I'm standing, it's because you knew it wasn't mine! Because you been fuckin' around with another nigga!"

"Judah, believe me, it's not what you think! That's what I'm trying to tell you!"

"It doesn't have to be what I think because I know what I saw! I watched another nigga drop you off with my own eyes, Jas! You can't lie your way out of this one!"

"Listen to me! I'm only with him because I—I—"

"You what?"

"I'm an undercover DEA agent investigating Bankx and his uncle, Big Rey!" she confirmed.

I shifted my weight from one leg to the other, unsure of what I had just heard. "Are you standing in my face right now tellin' me you the fuckin' Feds?"

She nodded. "Yes, but before you overreact, let me explain—"

I threw my hands up before charging for the bathroom door. "Nah! Fuck that! I'm out of here, yo!"

I scoffed. Skai had been right all along. I'd been too caught up living in the past, trying to relive the good times with my first love instead of seeing her for the woman she'd become, a woman I couldn't love.

She caught my hand at the knob. "Please wait and let me explain! Nothing between Bankx and me is real! It's all a front for my job, okay? He thinks my name is Bevin Watts. I—I'm a part of a task force between the DEA and the FBI. We want to take him down for murder, racketeering, trafficking, and so on. I needed him to trust me so I could get close enough to get information to indict him, but I swear, I don't love him! I put that on our son," she pleaded with tears in her eyes.

I twisted my neck to look at her. "And the baby?"

"It was yours; I swear! I haven't—"

"Then, why the fuck didn't you tell me?"

She wiped her eyes. "I—I don't know. I was scared and ashamed, but I couldn't process any of those feelings because of what I was sent here to do. I'm so close to wrapping this thing up, Ju. I know I am!"

"Yeah? And where does that leave my brothers and me, huh?"

"I promise I'm keeping you out of it. I don't want anything to happen to you."

"You're a fuckin' Fed, Jas! Why the fuck should I believe anything you say?"

"Because you know me!"

"I thought I did, but tonight only proved that I don't know a damn thing about you."

"I promise you; it's not you or your family that I'm after. But I can only speak for myself."

"What does that mean?"

"Do you know anyone by the name of Miguel Martinez?"

"That bitch ass FBI agent that's been fuckin' with my brothers and me for three fuckin' books now. What about him?"

"I think he's more invested in your family than he should be."

"In what way?"

"He's a part of the task force, and things have been off with him. I ignored it for a while, but things kept not adding up. So, I started doing my research."

"What did you find?"

"First, Miguel isn't his real first name. It's Alejandro Miguel Martinez Navarro, Jr. He changed his name before joining the FBI, shortening it to only go by his mother's surname so that no one would make the direct connection as to who his father was, Alejandro Miguel Martinez Navarro, Sr., the Columbian kingpin that was murdered years ago while here in the states," she revealed.

My brows twitched. "You tellin' me that fuckin' Fed is the son of a kingpin?"

"Yeah. Navarro was a Columbian national indicted on conspiracy charges and the intent to distribute drugs with a street value of over twelve million dollars. He remained a fugitive for over twenty years until we got word that he and his wife had been murdered."

"By who?"

"We aren't for certain. Could've been another drug lord or someone from inside his camp."

I slowly shook my head, careful not to let on that I knew exactly who she was talking about. Navarro was one of Big Rey's most ruthless rivals. The drug business was cutthroat, and niggas were always trying to take out the nigga ahead of 'em. Years ago, Big Rey had all of Navarro's goons murdered in the middle of the night before murdering him and his wife. He paid Bankx, Rome, and me handsomely to make sure no one ever found their bodies.

"That's all you found out?" I quizzed.

"For now. Do you know anything about any diamonds Bankx may have had?"

I shook my head and avoided her glance. "Diamonds? Nah, why?"

"Martinez mentioned something about diamonds in some paperwork I saw, but I haven't been able to track anything down."

"Why are you telling me all this?" I asked.

"Because I'm trying to prove that I'm telling the truth. I want to keep you as far away from this as possible."

"Yeah, well, if you think I'm finna stand here and help you solve your case, you got me fucked up," I assured her.

"Judah, please. This doesn't have to end like this. Now you know the truth. You know everything! We can start fresh; start clean. As soon as I wrap up this operation, we can—"

"What? Run off into the sunset together and act like none of this shit ever happened? My brother almost died on his wedding day behind that nigga, and you show up here telling me it's all pretend?"

"Yes! It's not real, Judah! None of it is real; it's just my job."

"Ain't shit about my life fake, Jasmin! None of it! And what does that say about us, huh? That was just your job too?"

"No! You know that was real. I meant it when I told you I loved you, Judah. I'm in this with you forever," she confessed, reaching out to grab my face.

I caught her hands in mid-air and lowered them. "Nah. Fool me once; shame on you. Fool me twice; shame on me."

"Judah, please!"

"Please? Please what? We were supposed to be seamless this time around, Jas. You don't know what I gave up for you. What I *fucked up* for you!"

"Things can be different. I just need a little more time!"

"You can have all the time you need. It won't matter."

"Why not?"

"Because I don't trust your ass, and I can't love someone I don't trust."

"Please don't go," she begged, grabbing my arm.

"If you meant any of the shit you said, I better not have no shit blowback on my family or me."

She shook her head. "It won't. We only want Big Rey and Bankx."

"Good, because I don't ever wanna see you or speak to your ass ever again."

BANKX

I PULLED A FRESH BLUNT FROM MY LIPS AND LOOKED DOWN AT MY phone just as it dinged with a text. "I've got the information you requested. Sending it to your email now," I mumbled aloud before swiping to open my email.

Inside was an unread message from the private investigator I'd hired to investigate Bevin. I walked over to my computer to download the zip file and saw photos of Bevin meeting with an FBI agent in different locations across *my* city. The last item in the file was a scanned newspaper clipping with a photo of her and Judah sporting youthful smiles and oversized velvet blue crowns with gold trim on their heads. Underneath the image was a description listing Judah Snow and Jasmin Baker as Westview Senior High School's 2010 homecoming king and queen. They both looked like babies to me. I was still trappin' in Atlanta at that time.

I airdropped the information to my cell and slammed my laptop shut. That goldmine of information should've been enough for me, but it wasn't. I was on a rampage to find out everything about her lying ass before I exposed her for the fraud she was. I thought back to the first instance that made me look into her in the first place; her random ass hospital stay. She claimed it was for appendicitis, but she waited days to call me and tell me about it. That shit never sat right with me.

I must've staked out in the hospital parking lot for hours before I peeped Skai making her way across the crosswalk and into the lot. I hopped out of my truck and dipped around the side to catch up to her on her left.

"Yo, Doc," I called out.

I watched her shoulders tense up from behind as she froze in her step. She slowly turned her neck in my direction before the rest of her body followed. "W—what are you doing here? What do you want?"

"I need you to do something for me."

She shook her head while trying to walk away from me. "I'm sorry, but I can't help you."

I blocked her way. "Tell me why my girl was really admitted into the hospital a few weeks ago."

"She's your girl, right? Why don't you ask her?" she suggested with a shrug.

"I'm asking you," I confirmed, brandishing the gun on my hip.

Her eyes widened. "Look, even if I wanted to tell you what you wanted to know, I couldn't. There's this thing called doctor-patient confidentiality. I could lose my license behind this," she informed me.

I pulled the gun away from my hip while pulling her close to me, so the gun was jammed right into her gut. "It's either your license or your life, and one really doesn't matter without the other, now does it?" I grumbled.

Her body quaked in my grasp, face growing warm with shame. "P—please don't make me do this."

"We can either march in that hospital with this gun aimed at you, or you can tell me what I wanna know right now. The quicker you decide, the sooner this can all be over, and you can go on about your night."

"O—okay, okay. I'll tell you whatever you wanna know; just p—please don't shoot me."

"Why the fuck was she really in the hospital? Was it for appendicitis, like she said?"

She slowly shook her head. "No. S—she had an ectopic pregnancy. We had to perform an emergency surgery, but the pregnancy was not viable in the end, and she lost the baby."

My eyes widened. "She was fuckin' pregnant?"

She swallowed hard. "P—please let me go. I told you all I know, now p—please let me go."

I glared at the woman trembling in front of me before slowly trailing the barrel of my chrome pistol from her navel up to the center of her chest. "I don't think I can do that."

In a daring attempt to escape, she shoved me back with all her might and tried to sprint to her car, but I caught her mid-stride and slapped my hand over her mouth. Her muffled screams sounded off into the palm of my hand while she struggled to break free from my grasp.

I pulled her keys from her grasp, quickly popped her trunk, and stuffed her petite frame inside. "Please don't do this! I don't know anything else! I swear!"

A sardonic smile flickered across my lips before I laughed down low in my throat. "It's nothin' personal, Doc. But to catch a fish, I gotta have bait," I replied before slamming the trunk lid shut. She may have been the last bargaining chip I had.

I hopped in her car and started the engine, fleeing the hospital lot as quickly as possible. Once I was sure we hadn't been followed, I tapped Bevin's name on my phone screen and placed it against my ear, listening to it ring five times before her voicemail took over. She'd proven what I'd already known to be true to some extent; a bitch could never fully be trusted. All that shit she'd preached about celibacy and waiting for the right moment when she was out here fuckin' niggas behind my back. I already knew she'd been meeting with the Feds, and now I had even more proof of what a liar she was. Whether her real name was Bevin Watts or Jasmin Baker, she was

K.L. Hall

nothing more than a beautiful snake in my garden that I'd have to cut the head off sooner than later.

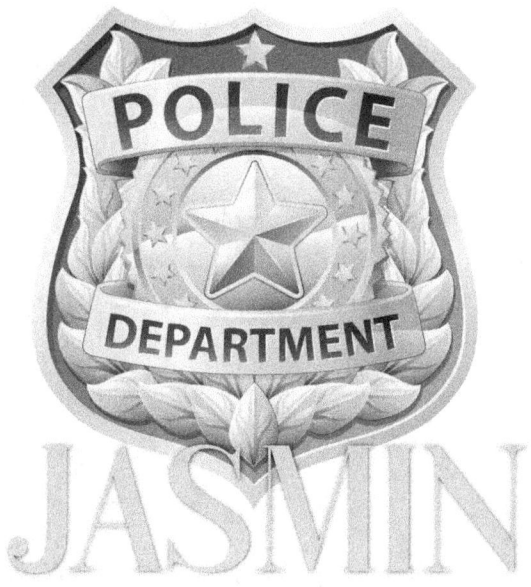

JASMIN

After scrubbing all the bugs I'd planted in and around Bankx's whereabouts, I'd *finally* gotten the last piece of evidence I needed to make an arrest and finally be able to put the case behind me. Judah had made it clear he didn't want anything else to do with me, and I had no choice but to respect it. The least I could do was get a win for my career. I played back a conversation between him and Big Rey discussing a drug shipment coming in tonight. Bankx thought there wasn't anyone capable of taking him down, and I was more than happy to prove him wrong. *I couldn't wait to see the look on his face once he realized his freedom had an expiration date.*

"This is our shot!" I cheered.

I darted to Miguel's office to share the news. After quickly surveying the room, I knew he wasn't there. There was a mahogany brown bookcase leaning against the wall with more books piled onto his long oak desk than the shelves. Messy manila folders were scattered across his desks, layered underneath unfinished cups of day-old coffee. It almost looked like he'd spent more time in his office than away from it. I darted across the worn sea-green carpet and wheeled his captain-style desk chair out of my way. I opened every drawer and file cabinet I could, searching for anything that would prove what I already knew to be true; Agent Martinez had a personal vendetta against Baby and his brothers. I tugged on his file cabinet drawer only to find it locked.

"Come on, come on," I mumbled, feeling around underneath mountains of paperwork for the key. I found it taped underneath his mousepad and quickly unlocked the drawers of his file cabinet.

"Oh shit!" I uncovered a bag of diamonds buried at the bottom of the drawer.

"Find whatever you're looking for?"

I snapped my neck toward the door to see Miguel standing with a scowl across his sienna-brown face. "Miguel—h—hey. I, uh, I thought I heard someone say you left for the day."

"Baker, what the fuck are you doing snooping around in my office?" he quizzed, arms folded across his barrel chest.

"Close the door," I told him.

He closed the door behind him while keeping his eyes trained on my hand. "What are you doing with those?"

"I came here to tell you I know when the next drop will be, but I found these in your file cabinet. Why aren't these in evidence?"

"I keep that drawer that locked for a reason, and besides, I told you I had a lot riding on this case, didn't I? I wanna keep them close."

I scoffed, "And I'm the one that's in too deep?" I asked, turning his revelation about me against him. "I know you wanna take these guys down. I do too, but there's a right and a wrong way to go about all this. I know you wanna do the right thing, and right now, whatever you're planning on doing with these isn't the right thing, and it isn't healthy, Miguel. We may not be friends, but I'm telling you this as your colleague. You're too close to this."

He pushed out an elongated sigh. "You're right. You're absolutely right. I'm sorry. I just wanna nail these mothafuckas so bad, and we're so close I can taste it. Just give me a chance to make it right, okay?"

I eyed him closely. "You need to put them where they need to be by tomorrow, or I'm going to tell your chief."

"Aight, yeah. I got you. When did you say the drop was gonna be?"

"It's tonight," I informed him.

Two and a half hours later, I hurried out of my apartment with my eyes glued to my phone. I had a missed call from Bankx and decided to call him back when I got in the car. I knew what was about to go down, and I wanted to be as close to the action as possible. I slammed my body into the driver's seat and reached out to start the engine when a voice sliced through the silence, letting me know I wasn't alone.

"You're right; I do wanna do the right thing."

I gasped. Eyes racing in a panic, I glanced into my rearview mirror and straight into Miguel's eyes. He'd positioned himself in my backseat. "Miguel, what the fuck?!" I yelled. "What are you doing in my car?"

"I couldn't say what I wanted to say in there."

"And what's that?"

"You're smart, Jasmin. I'll give you that. Too fuckin' smart for your own good."

A sudden deep frown creased my forehead. "What the hell is that supposed to mean?"

"Why did you have to turn your attention to me, huh? All you had to do was stay focused on Bankx, and things would've turned out according to plan, but now, things gotta change."

"So, what's your new plan? To run off with the diamonds and disappear as if no one will come looking for you?" I queried.

"That's exactly what I'm gonna do. They were my father's. Although nothing can replace his life, I had to get back what was rightfully his."

"What about the task force? You know they'll find out what you did."

"I wanted to see it all through. I promise I did, but justice is taking too fucking long, and now, I think I'll let those dogs devour themselves."

The look in his eyes made my skin quiver. They were hard and scornful.

"You know I can't let you get away with this, right?"

"I figured you'd say that, and that's why I know that doing the right thing means getting rid of you," he announced.

My spine tensed when he spoke the words. Before I could give a response, I felt a stinging, burning sensation across my throat. My hands shot up to cover his, trying my hardest to pull them away as he strangled me from behind. I slapped steering wheel, sounding off the horn as many times as possible before my vision became blurry and my limbs started to go numb, making it harder to fight.

"I'm sorry, but I'm too close to let you fuck this up," he confessed, breath fanning my skin as he squeezed my throat harder under I couldn't fight anymore. Hot tears welled in my eyes and a warm, calming sensation took over my body. I knew it was the end seconds before I pulled in my last breath, and everything went black.

BANKX

I CALLED BEVIN'S PHONE REPEATEDLY, READY TO EXPOSE HER FOR THE snake she was and put an end to her. Her line went to voicemail back-to-back until I arrived at her apartment in Skai's car, only to find the lot lit up with flashing red and blue lights and swarming with cops. That's when I knew something was up. I quickly pulled off to avoid being spotted, happy I hadn't pulled up in my truck. No one would be looking for me in Skai's car. Back on the highway and as far away from her place as I could be, I looked down to see that she was calling me back.

"Where you at?" I answered, "I just left your place."

The person on the other line replied, "Jarrell Carter, this is Agent Miguel Martinez."

I pulled the phone away from my ear. "The fuck?"

"Don't hang up. You want to talk to me, trust me."

"And why is that?"

"Because I've got your diamonds."

My brow creased, and my grip tightened around the phone. "What the fuck did you just say?"

"Oh, I think you heard me loud and clear. That's why you killed Jade Tran, isn't it?"

I scoffed. He was trying to bait me in, and I wasn't going to fall for it. "I don't know what the fuck you're talkin' about. I'm hanging up."

"They're yours for a price!" he called out.

I sucked my teeth while monitoring my rear and side mirrors to ensure I wasn't being followed. He didn't strike me as the type to want to negotiate over money; there was something more he wanted. "What do you want from me?"

"It's simple, really."

"Nothing is ever simple with the Feds," I reminded him.

"Give us Big Rey."

"Us?" I quizzed.

He let out a sinister chuckle. "I'm surprised you haven't asked about your girl yet. You aren't the least bit curious as to why we're speaking on her phone?"

"I had her followed. I know she met with you."

"Mmm."

After informing me of her death, he also confirmed that her real name was Jasmin Baker and that *bitch* was, in fact, an undercover DEA agent. There was an entire task force dedicated to stopping my uncle's entire operation and taking us both down. The next shipment of product was due to arrive in a few hours, and I knew she could've tipped him off about it before she died. I also knew she probably had my car, home, and phone tapped.

"Tell me something first," I negotiated.

"What?"

"The night I was picked up by the Feds. Who snitched?"

"An informant."

"That's not how this works, aight? I ask you a question, and it's your job to give me an answer. I need a name."

"I'm not playing your game."

"I guess we don't have shit else to discuss."

"Fine! Wait! I don't have your file in front of me. You'll have to give me a minute or two to get that information."

"You know the number to dial when you do," I stated before ending the call.

With the windows cracked and music loud to drown out her screams, I pushed Skai's car down the interstate. Ten minutes later, I got a text with the name Zachary Palmer just before my phone rang again.

"Yeah?" I answered.

"You get the text?"

"I did."

"Well, then, you got your answer."

"Zachary fuckin' Palmer," I mumbled, knowing exactly who he was.

The snitch was one of my uncle's hittas who would've done whatever he said to do whenever he said to do it. Besides me, my uncle was the only one who knew my route that night because I was making a special delivery for him. That was all the proof I needed to know that my uncle was the one who'd set me up with his product, knowing I would be too loyal to do anything but do my time and keep my fuckin mouth shut. All these years, he'd been hiding behind Rome and his brother as the ones who set me up when it was him all along. As badly as I wanted to know why he did it, deep down, I knew it didn't matter. All that mattered to me now was payback.

"Oh, and did I mention that if you *don't* agree to help me take your uncle down, I *will* pin Agent Baker's murder on you, and trust me; I've got enough to make it stick," he warned.

We both knew her blood wasn't on my hands, but none of that mattered. All that mattered was that she was a dead Fed who had ties to me.

As mad as I was that I didn't get a chance to confront her, I reminded myself I was still driving around with Skai in my possession. My wheels started turning. I needed to get my diamonds and get to international waters, but the only way to do that was to snitch on the man who'd arranged to have my freedom taken from me. The last bit of family I had didn't give a fuck about me, so he could rot in hell for the rest of his life for all I cared.

"Before I agree to anything, I want proof that you have what's mine," I stated.

"Coming your way. Stand by."

I received a text a few seconds later and opened it to see a photo of the diamonds. My eyes danced with joy. "Fine. I'll tell you what you wanna know after you give me my diamonds," I declared, agreeing the give him whatever information he needed about my uncle's operation in exchange for the diamonds.

"When can we meet?" I asked, eager to get the fuck out of the city.

"You tell me."

With my uncle out of the way, I only had a few more loose ends to tie up before I kissed the States goodbye for good.

"I take it you already know what's goin' to happen in a few hours. Let's handle our business outside, and then you take down whoever you gotta take down inside," I reasoned, planning to set up Baby and Rome.

"Will Big Rey be there?"

"No, but some other high-level distros will be."

"Who? Who's gonna be there?"

"I'm sure the name Roman Snow has come across your radar. Nigga and his brother movin' big weight," I informed him.

"I'm familiar," he growled. "How sure are you that he'll be there?"

"Positive."

"If you cross me, I will personally push for you to get the death penalty for Agent Baker's murder," he threatened.

"You and I both know I ain't have shit to do with that."

"That's my word against yours. Which one of us do you think the judge will believe?" he warned.

"He'll be there," I reiterated, a hint of annoyance in my voice.

"He better be, or I'll make sure Big Rey knows exactly which one of his loyal soldiers snitched on him. How do you think he'll feel when he finds out his nephew's a criminal informant?"

I shrugged before darting my eyes toward the rearview mirror.

"Not my problem. Besides, payback is a bitch," I replied before ending the call and tossing my phone out of the window.

I'd managed to arrange the perfect ambush. I'd siphon money from those bitch-ass niggas in exchange for Skai and get my diamonds back from the Feds. After I got what I needed, I'd become a ghost in the wind, and the Feds would take the Snow brothers down in the process. It wasn't death but ripping them away from everyone they loved would be the cherry on top for me. All I had to do was sit back, relax, and enjoy the show from across international waters.

I pulled over into a large lot and popped the trunk. Trembling, Skai looked up to see my gun aimed at the middle of her forehead. "What's up, Doc?"

"P—please let me go," she pleaded, lips trembling around her words.

I watched the river of tears flowing down her sunken cheeks and my mouth jerked to a grin. "Gladly. Give me your phone. It's time we call your boyfriend."

BABY

AFTER OFFICIALLY ENDING EVERYTHING BETWEEN JASMIN AND ME, I reached out to Skai, ready to tell and show her how serious I was about giving us a real shot. After a lot of back and forth, she'd finally agreed to meet me for dinner so that we could talk things out face-to-face and see if she'd be willing to give things another try. I started blowing up her phone when she didn't show up at the restaurant after an hour. It wasn't until I drove past the hospital, scouring the lot for her car, that my phone rang. My eyes darted to the screen, relieved when I saw her name pop up on the screen.

"Skai?! Hello? Where you at? I've been waiting on you for over an hour," I answered in a huff. My blood ran cold when I heard Bankx laugh on the other end of the phone. "Touch her, and I'll show you something worse than death," I warned him.

"I remember seeing pictures of the two of you looking really cozy at your brother's wedding. I know you got history with Jasmin, too, but how much is this one worth to you?"

"What the fuck do you want?!" I barked into the receiver, blood pressure inching to dangerous levels.

"I want my fuckin' diamonds back, boy!" he shouted back.

"I ain't got your diamonds, nigga!"

"Then again, you tell me how much this bitch is worth to you. Let's start the bidding at, let's say, half a million. Yeah. Half a million plus the money for the drugs when we meet for the drop," he demanded.

I frowned. "What? That's in a few hours. I can't move that type of money in that short amount of time!"

"The clock is ticking. Bodies are dropping like flies around the city tonight," he warned before hanging up in my face.

I was sick to my stomach knowing Bankx had Skai in his possession. I wouldn't be able to live with myself if she got hurt behind being involved with me. I knew he was only using her as a pawn to bring me to my knees. He'd felt like he had the absolute upper hand after Big Rey named him his new frontrunner and was throwing all his weight around because of it. I couldn't wait to pluck the crown from his head.

After informing Rome and Chief about Bankx's demands and that he had Skai, I scrambled to come up with the money to get Skai back. An hour passed, and I got a text from Skai's phone with a link to a news clip about an undercover DEA agent's body being found and clicked it to see Jasmin's photo show up. My eyes scanned the article, unable to process that Jasmin had been killed, when another text came in.

> New meet-up location. Salvage yard on 47th
> Street. Drive to the back.

Changing the meeting location let me know he was taunting me, baiting me in, and waiting for me to fail.

"I don't like it," Rome grumbled, shaking his head.

"It could be an ambush," Chief added.

"I don't trust it either, but what other choice do we have? He has Skai. I'll lose my mind if anything happens to her," I told them.

"Don't worry, she's gonna be okay," Chief assured me.

Rome nodded. "We gon' get her back."

Just before we were about to leave, Chief's phone rang. "It's Gianna," he announced, eyes on the screen. He walked away to answer it and returned with his face as pale as a ghost. "Something's wrong. I gotta get to the hospital."

"Do your thing. We can handle this," I assured him.

Rome drove the car through the gate surrounded by tall chain-link fencing topped with barbed wire to deter theft from the salvage yard. It was late, so there was no attendant at the entrance and no one inside scavenging for parts. The tires of his Mercedes made tracks across the dusty earth, kicking up rocks, loose screws, and other debris in their wake as we rode to the back of the yard. We passed by dozens of broken-down vehicles with raised hoods, some with wires and hoses sprouting out of the top like weeds.

"There's her car right there!" I pointed out to him.

Rome placed the car in park and kept the engine running. I hopped out, ready to face Bankx head-on. "Where the fuck is she!" I exploded.

Bankx stood tall, stance widened. "Where's my money, nigga?"

I clenched my jaw. "I'm not the mothafucka you wanna play with," I warned him. "Now, tell me where the fuck she is before I get to bussin' out this mothafucka!"

"All that shit you talkin', you better be prepared to stand on your word, *boy,*" he forewarned, brandishing the two guns on his hip.

"I ain't never been afraid to pull the trigger, nigga. I'll stick a fuckin' fork in you! Remember that!" I threatened right back.

Rome inched a few steps ahead of me and tossed two large duffel bags so that they landed at Bankx's feet. "Here's the money. It's all there. The cut for the product and half a million for Skai. Cold, hard cash, like you asked."

He stepped forward to retrieve the bags. "Nice doing business with you," he grumbled before tossing me the keys to Skai's car.

I popped the trunk and raced to her car to make sure she was okay. As soon as I got to her, Agent Martinez jumped out and started shooting at us.

"Freeze! Put your fuckin' hands up!"

One of his bullets hit Rome, taking him down. "Ahh, shit!" he cried out in pain.

"Stay down and stay here!" I directed Skai. "I'll come back for you."

The shootout ensued as I raced to Rome's side to learn he'd only been grazed, but his right leg was still wounded. Staying low, I pulled him to safety behind his car door, using it as a shield.

I stood up to shoot when I caught a bullet to the shoulder and another to my right side, causing me to tumble to the ground, landing on my elbow before my back hit the dust. Agent Martinez raced over to me, gun aimed as he stood over me. "I can't wait to put a bullet in your ass," he grumbled.

I heard the safety click on another gun just before he pulled the trigger. Bankx was standing behind him, gun aimed at the back of his dome. "Give me one reason I shouldn't let him finish your ass off," he told me.

"Because he ain't who he says he is!"

"What's he talkin' about?" Bankx asked Agent Martinez.

"His name is Alejandro Miguel Martinez Navarro, Jr.! His father was Alejandro Miguel Martinez Navarro, Sr.! The Columbian kingpin that Big Rey murdered years ago!"

I knew the name had to ring a bell. Big Rey had his crew take out all of Navarro's men before assassinating him and his wife execution-style, then had Bankx, Rome, and I get rid of the bodies.

"Are you serious?"

"I'm tellin' the truth! Jasmin was looking into him. She told me everything!"

"You're the son of a kingpin?" Bankx asked him for confirmation.

"He's right. But what neither of you knows is not only did Reynard

205

Shaw murder both of my parents, but he stole my father's diamonds. These diamonds," he revealed, pulling them out of his pocket.

As a distraction, he dropped the bag to the ground, letting all ten diamonds fall out and dance across the ground before spinning around to turn his gun on Bankx. Before he could pull the trigger, Bankx sent a bullet straight into his chest, and we watched his body hit the ground.

"If it's one thing I hate, it's a crooked mothafuckin' Fed, especially one that ain't on my payroll," he grumbled.

I hurried to my feet as quickly as I could. "Don't think you did me no favors," I stated while raising my gun to him. "This shit ain't over. You and I both know it ain't gon' end until one of us is dead!" I yelled, hand covering the bullet hole in my side. The louder I raised my voice, the more blood leaked out.

He glanced down at the diamonds scattered at the agent's feet. "I ain't leavin' here until I get what I came for, so if you gon' shoot me, you gon' have to shoot me in my mothafuckin' back," he stated before reaching down to pick up as many scattered diamonds as he could. The minute he rose to his feet, Rome stood with his gun aimed at his head.

"Nah, I want you to know I was the one who took your last breath," Rome gritted, finger wrapped around the trigger.

Amid the ambush, word exchanges, and shootout, Rome had managed to make his way from behind the car door to a spot where he could approach Bankx from behind. Even on his knees with a gun aimed at his dome, Bankx continued to taunt him. "Pull it then, mothafucka. You got the heart to do it, then finish me off, bitch nigga!"

"Then die, mothafucka," Rome's voice boomed from behind.

Multiple gunshots rang out before Bankx's body dropped to the ground in two separate but equally loud thuds. He leaned down to scrape up the diamonds before we saw headlights and heard the rumbling of an engine nearby. After all the gunfire ceased, Skai had climbed out of the trunk and was waiting in the driver's seat, ready to get us all the hell out of dodge. Rome and I made our way to the car, limping and in pain.

"Let's get in my car, and I'll drive. You take care of my brother," Rome suggested.

"You're hurt too!" Skai hollered in a panic.

"It's just a flesh wound. I'll be okay."

The three of us made our way to Rome's car, and I piled into the backseat, leaking blood all over his interior as Skai tried her best to provide aid.

"Are you okay?" she asked, swiping her hand down my face.

"Don't worry about me. Are you okay?"

"Shh. Don't waste your breath. It's gonna be okay. We're gonna get you to the hospital!" she assured me.

As soon as we hit the interstate, we saw a swarm of red and blue lights heading the way we'd just come. Martinez must've let them know that an intended drop was going down, but they were too late. By the time they got there, the only thing they'd find were two dead bodies.

SKAI

AND IN THE END, WE WERE ALL SAFE.

We got to the hospital, and I ensured Ju and Rome were checked out. Rome's wound was patched up, and Ju underwent surgery to remove the bullet fragments and was held for observation. I stayed by his side the entire time, anxious for the anesthesia to wear off so that he'd wake up and I could thank him for saving my life. I put the tray of untouched food on the table at his bedside and walked over to the window with a bouquet of fresh flowers in my hand.

"I see you ended up patching me up after all," his groggy voice stated from behind me.

I twisted my neck as a smile shaped my mouth. "Actually, it wasn't me. They don't let you operate on people you...well, I'm glad you're okay."

"Come here," he insisted.

I inched closer to his side. "How are you feeling?"

"Heart still beating, so I guess I ain't got no right to complain."

I pushed out a long sigh. "I don't think I've ever been so scared in my life. Watching you take those bullets like that. Jesus, your body has limits, y'know?"

He dipped his chin. "I do, but you see, I'm alright."

"You're one of the lucky ones. Don't you think it's time to slow down, take a step back and find a new path?"

"That depends."

"On what?" I quizzed.

"If that path involves you."

Before I could respond, there was a quick knock on the door before we were joined by the other two Snow brothers and company. "We can finish talking later. I'll give you time with your family."

He reached out to grab my hand, interlocking our fingers. "Stay," he insisted.

Chief walked over to give his brother a long hug and then announced that he and Gianna had welcomed a healthy baby boy a few hours prior. He was a preemie but expected to graduate from the NICU and be able to leave the hospital by the end of the week. Rome, Lira, and their son approached Ju next, all sharing hugs, grateful that he was alive. I stayed parked by his side until they left, and it was just the two of us again. The room that had once been filled with various voices and laughter had suddenly fallen silent.

"Yo, remember that dream you told me you had when we were in Jamaica?" he asked.

"Barely, but yeah."

"It wasn't a dream."

My brows knitted. "What do you mean?"

"What I said to you was real. I was fuckin' crazy about you then, and I still am."

My forehead knotted in confusion, halfway not believing the words coming out of his mouth. "Ju, I don't think now is the best time to—"

He blurted out his confession, "There's somethin' I've wanted to say to you since before all this shit went down. I'm sorry it took all of this to get us face-to-face, but I gotta get this off my chest."

"There's something I've been wanting to say to you too."

"Since I'm the one laid up in the hospital bed, let me go first, aight?"

"Okay."

"I'm sorry, Skai. I hate knowing I fucked everything up between us, and I hate knowing that I could've been who you needed me to be, and I chose not to be because I was too afraid to deal with my past. It's fucked with me every day since, and I put that on my son. I want to make you mine, for real, this time. No games. No excuses. Just you and me. My timing ain't never been perfect, but I *do* love you. You think you can find it in your heart to forgive me so we can start over?"

"What else can I say but yes to the man who saved my life?" I asked, wiping tears from my eyes.

He let out a soft chuckle before pulling my hand to his lips to kiss my knuckle. "Well, in that case, I don't think I've ever been so happy to get shot. I meant it when I said there is nothing I won't do to protect you, Skai. The limit does not exist when it comes to you."

Hearing his words made me realize I couldn't see my life without him in it. It would be like asking me to go without food, water, or even air.

I stroked a finger against his cheek. "I don't want you out of my life, Ju. I've been walking around trying to instill into my brain that I don't need you and I don't love you, but all I could think about after seeing you shot was that there's no way I wanna be without you. I tried to move on, but nobody is you. You're the only one I want."

"I'm ready to hear it now," he stated.

"Hear what?"

"You tell me you love me."

A smile flickered at the edge of my mouth before I stood on the tips of my toes to lean over the rail. We locked eyes, and our lips met. "I love you, Judah Snow."

"I love you, too."

SKAI

Six weeks later.

I stepped out of the hospital on my lunch break, quickly flashing my badge at Norman, the security guard, when my phone rang. I placed the phone to my ear as I headed out to my car.

"Hello?"

"Skai?"

I froze. The person on the other line had a voice that sounded like Jade's but different like it had been altered somehow. "W–who is this?"

"Turn around and see for yourself," she insisted.

Following her instructions, I turned my neck to see Jade walking my way and couldn't believe my eyes. My knees turned to water. I had to be seeing a ghost. She lowered the phone from her ear while continuing to make her way toward me.

"I'm glad you didn't change your number. It's the only one I had memorized," she uttered, standing an arms-length away from me.

"I—is this real?" I whispered to her, still unwilling to believe my eyes.

"It's me," she confirmed, clutching my arm.

I gave her a once-over before reaching out to hug her. I took a silent sigh of relief when her body pressed against mine. She was real. The moment was really happening. "Oh my God! I can't believe it's you. I can't believe you're here. I have so many questions! Where have you been all this time? How did you survive? D—does Ba know you're back?"

She shook her head. "No one knows yet but you. You were the first person I wanted to see. I remember you being there in the alley that night. I thought I was going to die, but then you showed up. You saved my life, Skai."

My eyes misted with tears as I tightened my arms around her. "What? H—how? I just knew I was too late! You'd already lost so much blood."

"I don't remember much, but an FBI agent was in my room when I woke up after surgery."

My eyes widened. "Agent Martinez?"

"Yeah. How'd you know?" she quizzed.

"Long story. Keep going."

"He told me I had to undergo hours of emergency surgery and a blood transfusion, but luckily the cut hadn't completely severed my vocal cords. There I was, happy to be alive and shit, and then he told me I was facing a three-year prison sentence for aggravated identity theft and some more shit. He forced me to agree to testify against Bankx in the federal case they were building against him."

My mind continued to race, one fleeting, jumbled thought after another. "All this time, I thought you were dead!"

"I'm sorry. I love you. I would've reached out if I could've, but I didn't want to put you in any more danger."

"So much has happened since you've been gone! Bankx is dead, and so is Agent Martinez," I informed her.

"I know. That's why I was allowed to leave the safe house they were holding me in and return to Miami. There's no more case."

Although Bankx and Agent Martinez were dead, the Feds still managed to finally take down Big Rey, indicting him on multiple charges of murder, conspiracy, trafficking, and more.

"I know. It was all over the news a couple of weeks ago. But now that it's over, is that it? Y–you're free to go?"

She scoffed. "If you consider probation for the next three years free, then yeah."

"Probation for what?"

She shrugged. "You know I was doing my dirt outside of Bankx. Somehow, they found out I'd been stealing credit card information from clients at Ba's shop and threatened to shut his business down. I couldn't risk having Ba lose everything behind me, so I had no choice but to agree to take the deal and testify."

"So, that's how Agent Martinez got the diamonds?"

"Yeah. I stashed the diamonds before Bankx could get to me. When he realized I didn't have them, he chased me down the alleyway and slit my throat. After the doctors cleared me to leave the hospital, I was escorted to the FBI field office in Tallahassee for questioning, and as part of my deal to get full immunity after the trial, I told him where I'd stashed the diamonds."

I reached out for her hand, rubbing comforting circles over it. "I'm so sorry you had to go through that."

"I would've gotten immunity had there been a trial to testify at, but it is what it is. All that matters is I have my life back. Nothing can replace that."

I stared at her in awe. "I still can't believe you're back."

She cheesed, doing a whole spin. "In the flesh, baby!"

"What's the plan now? Because I know you've got one."

"Of course I do. I'm done with that life. I'm going legit to focus on my dancing. Maybe get back into school or something."

I let out a sigh of relief, happy to hear she'd had a change of heart. Ju and I were truly free to be together and live our lives without looking over our shoulders, and I had my best friend back.

"I'm just so glad you're back," I expressed, pulling her into my arms for what felt like the hundredth time.

She wrapped her arms around me. "Best bitches for life?"
A smile crinkled my mouth. "Best bitches for life."
THE END

A note from K.L. Hall.

Reader,

Thank you for reading the final book in the Heist of Hearts series and Baby and Skai's love story. If you've made it this far, I hope you'll consider taking a minute to tell me what you thought about the book in the form of a **book review and/or rating**. Don't hesitate to let me know what you'd like to see from me next! I thoroughly enjoy reading your thoughts and hearing from you as well! I'm always striving to attract new readers and retain current ones, and reviews are one of the easiest ways to attract readers. If you loved the book, tell a friend, and most importantly, let me know!

All my love,
    K.L. Hall

Book discussion bonus.

Loved the book and want to get the conversation started? Try these free book discussion builders.

1. What was your favorite part of the book?
2. What was your least favorite?
3. Which scene stuck with you the most?
4. Which plot twist surprised you the most?
5. Rate the "heat" level of the book on a scale from 1-10. Ten being the hottest.
6. Was Skai and Baby's connection believable? If so, at what point did they click for you?
7. Who would you cast as the leads if you were making a movie of this book?
8. Share your favorite quote from the book. Why did this quote stand out?

About the Author

K.L. Hall is a national bestselling and award-winning author. As a serial storyteller, Hall has penned over three dozen titles in various genres—including African American urban fiction and romance, paranormal, children's books (as Kimberley M.), and non-fiction. Her fictional stories straddle the intersection of classic Urban and spellbinding Romance.

Highly Acclaimed Titles:

In the Arms of a Savage: (Peaked at #1 in Women's Fiction)

Fallin' for the Alpha of the Streets: (Peaked at #4 in Women's Fiction)

The Solace Series (Peaked at #1 and #2 in African American Erotica)

Sign up for my mailing list to stay up to date with new releases, giveaways, sneak peeks, and more! Click this link: https://bit.ly/38RMpV5 (*E-Book Only*)

Connect with me on social media:

Facebook: https://www.facebook.com/authorklhall
 Twitter: https://twitter.com/authorklhall
 Instagram: https://www.instagram.com/officialklhall/
 Website: https://www.authorklhall.com

Other novels by K.L. Hall:

Diary of a Hood Princess 1-3

Rise of a Street King: The Justice Silva Story (*Spin-Off to the Diary of a Hood Princess series*)

Where He Belongs: A Disrespectful Love Story

Love Me Harder: A Sin City Love Story

Broken Condoms and Promises 1-3

In the Arms of a Savage 1-3

Built for a Savage: Blaze and Camille's Love Story (*Spin-Off to the In the Arms of a Savage Series*)

A Ruthle$$ Love Story 1-3

Fallin' for the Alpha of the Streets 1-2

The Most Savage of Them All: The Wolfe Calloway Story (*Prequel to the In the Arms of a Savage Series*)

When a Gangsta Loves a Good Girl

Caught Between my Husband and a Hustler

The Illest Taboo 1-2

To the Only Thug I'll Ever Love

A Lover's Heist: Chief and Gianna's Love Story

A Lover's Heist II: Rome and Lira's Love Story

A Lover's Heist III: Baby and Skai's Love Story

Novellas:

Bi-Curious: An Erotic Tale

Bi-Curious 2: Tastes Like Candy

House of Cards 1-2

A Savage Calloway Christmas (*Christmas novella to the In the Arms of a Savage Series*)

Lovin' the Alpha of the Streets: A Valentine's Day Novella (*Valentine's Day novella to the Fallin' for the Alpha of the Streets Series*)

Awakened: A Paranormal Romance

As Long as You Stay Down

Solace in Seven

Solace II: The Final Cut

Children's Books:

Princess for Hire

Princess Twinkle Toes & the Missing Magic Sneakers

Little One, Change the World

Adjust Your Crown: A Self-Love Coloring Book for Children of Color

Non-Fiction:

Authors are a Business: The Booked & Busy Course Mini Book